"Did you want me as a *wife*, Max? The family deal? A wife and . . . and . . ."

"Well, hell, yes. Any way I could get you."

She blinked, looking stricken.

"Now, wait a minute, Gracie." He took a step toward her, his hand extended. "I didn't mean that it was just about sex."

"What was it about, then?"

He went with the truth, for lack of a better alternative. "We got married because we were in love, Gracie. I mean completely, gonzo, in love."

"*Were?*" she repeated tremulously.

He moved his hand a few inches to brush his fingers along her forearm. "Try me, Gracie," he said.

"I already have."

He covered her hand with his, leaned down, touched her hair. "Yeah, well, try me again."

"Max . . ." she said, almost a whisper.

He rested a hand on the back of the chair and moved in to fit their mouths together.

It had been too long. Way too long. He clasped her head, tilting it up to press their mouths closer. She clutched his sleeve, and heat rolled up Max's body in a wave of solid sensuality that could have lit brush fires.

This wasn't just a kiss, he realized with rapidly dissipating coherence. This was Grace. Max Hogan didn't kiss Grace Bennet Hogan as a casual gesture. Two seconds' contact and it was out of control.

WHAT ARE *LOVESWEPT* ROMANCES?

They are stories of true romance and touching emotion. We believe those two very important ingredients are constants in our highly sensual and very believable stories in the LOVE-SWEPT line. Our goal is to give you, the reader, stories of consistently high quality that may sometimes make you laugh, sometimes make you cry, but are always fresh and creative and contain many delightful surprises within their pages.

Most romance fans read an enormous number of books. Those they truly love, they keep. Others may be traded with friends and soon forgotten. We hope that each LOVESWEPT romance will be a treasure—a "keeper." We will always try to publish

LOVE STORIES YOU'LL NEVER FORGET
BY AUTHORS YOU'LL ALWAYS REMEMBER

The Editors

EX AND FOREVER

LINDA
WARREN

BANTAM BOOKS
NEW YORK · TORONTO · LONDON · SYDNEY · AUCKLAND

EX AND FOREVER
A Bantam Book / March 1997

ISBN 0-553-44576-6

Published simultaneously in the United States and Canada

Bantam Books are published by Bantam Books, a division of Bantam Doubleday Dell Publishing Group, Inc. Its trademark, consisting of the words "Bantam Books" and the portrayal of a rooster, is Registered in U.S. Patent and Trademark Office and in other countries. Marca Registrada. Bantam Books, 1540 Broadway, New York, New York 10036.

PRINTED IN THE UNITED STATES OF AMERICA
OPM   10 9 8 7 6 5 4 3 2 1

ONE

It had been one month, three weeks, and six days since Max Hogan had seen his soon-to-be ex-wife. He was over her.

"Absolutely," he told Ernie, who was downing a beer at the Blue Moon, on the late-night side of a Friday shift.

"Is that a fact?" Ernie said. He was still in uniform. When he set his glass down, the handcuffs on his belt clinked, punctuating the comment.

Max glanced at himself in the dim mirror behind the bar. Did he look like he was making it up? Five o'clock shadow on his jaw, black leather jacket with a new scuff at the elbow, bandage across his knuckles, courtesy of a switchblade with a bad attitude. He scowled. What did what he looked like have to do with it, anyway? "Yeah," he said to Ernie. "It's a fact."

"I gotta admire your style, Maxwell," Ernie drawled. "Not many men who've been dumped by a woman like Gracie would be able to take it in stride. But you—you just throw yourself into your work, take all the P.I. cases no one else'll touch. 'Course, you may not live a normal life span, but you'll have a hell of a reputation as a private investigator when you go out."

"You making some kind of point here, Ernie?"

"Some kind of point?" Ernie said innocently. "About your ex-wife, you mean? Grace?"

How many exes was he supposed to have? Max thought. One had been nearly enough to kill him. "I don't really want to talk about it," he said.

"Funny. That's not what Betty told me last week."

"Betty?"

"That blond rookie detective who's been trying to get your attention? The one who drove you to the hospital to get those stitches in your hand? Those were her very words. 'He sure doesn't have any trouble talking about his ex-wife, does he?' "

Max frowned. Betty? He'd thought her name was Patty.

"She's cute, that detective," Ernie went on, taking Max's silence as an invitation to keep talking. "Doesn't have Grace's eyes, though. Those dark brown eyes."

Max's fist closed around the neck of his beer bottle.

"You know," Ernie said, "sometimes a man needs more than cute."

Max felt that odd, inexplicable tightening in his chest that plagued him whenever he was blindsided by a mention of his ex-wife. He knew about Grace's soft brown eyes, how a man could fall into that sweet, liquid gaze, let his pain go, lose himself in those eyes, sell his soul for them.

And then where was he? Soulless, that's where. No. Max didn't need anything more than cute. He'd given up on needs. Needs were something you had to figure out, and understand, and next thing you knew you were drinking beer in places where the background music was songs about losing your woman and becoming a desperado.

"You know, Maxwell," Ernie said, "for a man whose marriage broke up over an extraneous saleslady in a new hot tub, you sure haven't seen much circulation since you've been single."

Max muttered something and snagged a couple of pretzels in his one good hand. The pretzels were supper, a meal he'd forgotten in the process of apprehending a slippery check forger and delivering him to Ernie for booking—a favor he wasn't getting much thanks for.

"Was she a blonde?"

"Who?" Max asked, confused for a minute. Grace was a brunette, with the kind of pale, pearl-smooth, luminous skin that was softer than suede, sweeter than the delicate underside of a shell. He'd imagined the way it would have looked, viewed through the shimmering water of a hot tub . . .

"The one Grace caught you with in the hot tub."

"Oh." He scowled again at Ernie. "That one. I didn't notice."

"You didn't notice? You get caught in a hot tub with another woman and you don't know if she's a blonde?"

"I didn't get *caught* in the hot tub, Ernie, because there wasn't anything to catch. For Pete's sake, I've told you that before. The woman was part of the installation crew. She was trying to sell me an extended warranty."

"Oh." Ernie looked at him sideways. "Must've been the fact that she was in the hot tub that threw me off."

Max drained his beer and banged the bottle down on the bar. All the nerve endings in his injured knuckles sent up a violent clamor designed to make him sorry. He let go of the bottle and gave his hand a shake, grimacing.

Grace hadn't wanted to hear any explanations about the saleslady in the new hot tub. She'd steered the argument right into the deep issues, sliding over the champagne, the bikini, and Max's reasonable explanations about why he thought she'd be delighted when he surprised her on their first anniversary with a newly installed hot tub.

She'd been surprised, all right. Especially by the saleslady in the bikini.

"So what'd she say?" Ernie asked, shifting and clinking his handcuffs again.

Max sighed. "She said, 'You're just not ready for marriage, Max.' "

"Oh," Ernie said, looking pained. "Yeah, well . . ."

Yeah, well. It was one of those conjugal arguments that came tailor-fitted with its own evidence. Hell, if he'd been ready for marriage, he would have had some clue about why splurging all his savings on an anniversary gift for his wife could lead directly to a marital inquisition about his character, attitude, and family values.

He *hadn't* been ready, he had to admit, either for the argument or for marriage. When he'd married Grace, he hadn't even known which end of the wedding cake was up. And heading out for the honeymoon, he sure as hell hadn't been thinking about a piece of the rock.

The jukebox clicked, then started crooning again. *This band of gold will keep me chained to you.* Something kind of off-key and scratchy about it, though . . . Oh, Ernie was humming along with the tune.

"You mind, Ernie? Not singing in my ear about wedding rings?"

"Oh, yeah," Ernie said. "I was just figuring you were over Gracie by now."

"I am."

"That's good, Max. 'Cause I figure you're about out of luck with all those high-risk jobs you've been taking to keep your mind off her."

Max frowned and grabbed another handful of pretzels. "I haven't been offered any fluff jobs lately."

"What about that last one—the one from Grace's aunt?"

"The stolen bottle job?"

"Yeah. The fluff job. One that'll pay a lot of money and not involve any appreciable risk. How come you're not taking that one?"

"You gotta be kidding. I told you. That's not a job. It's a *setup*, Ernie. That's nothing but Aunt Busybody Lillian trying to get me involved in some scheme."

"Yeah," Ernie said. "Lillian's one hell of a devious woman." The comment sounded like a compliment. "So what is it this time? Getting Grace to take you back?"

. . . *Getting Grace to take him back.* Another little twist was added to the knot in Max's chest. Lillian trying to get them back together. Some unruly, crazy hope spurted through him before he tackled it and got it down.

The only problem with the Lillian-to-the-rescue scenario was that Lillian's last attempt to salvage his marriage had backfired big time, and cost him a fortune to boot, which he hadn't really been able to afford, not after the hot tub.

His ex-wife didn't want him back. Grace had made that clear. Crystal clear, you might say. And he'd paid for the crystal.

"It's not gonna work, Ernie."

"Is that a fact?"

"Absolutely. And I'm not taking Lillian's job."

"Well, it's your call, Maxwell."

Conversation ceased for a minute, replaced by the sound of munching and the background throb of the jukebox.

"You ever think, Maxwell, that maybe it's not a fluff job?"

"What—Lillian's idea?"

"You know, could be that that bottle she wants you to check out, that—What is it?"

"A bitters flask. A Jacob's Ladder historical bitters flask."

"Yeah, well, you know about that more than I do."

He ought to know, Max thought. His future ex-wife bought, sold, located, and auctioned them, and Max had investigated the history of more than one in the interest of her antiques business. Grace's aunt Lillian, on the other hand, knew squat about historical bottles, or any other kind of antique. "Ernie," Max said, "Lillian hates antiques. Her idea of old is pre-1990s. What would she know about some antique bottle Grace is selling?"

"I don't know," Ernie said. "Still, Lillian gets around in all kinds of circles. Maybe she heard something. Could be it really *is* stolen."

"No way. Grace wouldn't be handling the sale if it was stolen. No. She would have turned down the commission."

"Unless she didn't know."

"Grace knows her business, Ernie."

"Yeah. But sometimes, a guy who's selling something like that can be real . . . persuasive, you know?"

"What do you mean, persuasive? You mean *persuasive?* Are you trying to make me jealous?"

"It's not much of a challenge, Max."

"It's not going to work, Ernie."

"Is that a fact?"

Hello walls, the jukebox sang. *Have you seen her lately?*

"You know," Ernie continued, "you do come across something in the computer files every once in a while about antiques fraud. Usually involves some good-looking con man takin' advantage of some honest dealer's good nature. You know, especially if the dealer is . . . single."

Max let out a sigh and pinched the bridge of his nose, feeling the knot in his chest convolute itself into a double-tied, triple-wrapped hangman's noose. "You know, Ernie, sometimes I wonder what life would be like if I didn't have you watching out for me."

"Damn right. Just do me a favor, Max. Stay out of the law enforcement computer banks when you check it out, okay? You need illegally obtained information, do it the old-fashioned way, huh? Bribe a cop."

The front doorbell chimed.

Grace Hogan's goldfish froze halfway to the surface, opened his mouth as if to suck in one of the flakes floating inches above him, then went into sudden, quivering, vibrating ecstasy.

Grace stared at him, transfixed, the box of fish flakes in her hand. "Lucifer?" she murmured. "What's the matter with you?" She touched the side of the crystal punch bowl. The faint, resonating chime of the glass fell silent, and Lucifer stopped vibrating.

It had to be some kind of auditory response, Grace realized. A reaction to the sounds or the vibrations of the door chime, some tremor in the crystal, that gave Lucifer an intensely . . . sensual experience. Her goldfish was gobbling fish flakes as if he'd depleted all his energy and wanted to build it up in a hurry, in case the opportunity for depletion came again.

It did. The doorbell chimed a second time.

Alarmed, Grace wrapped both hands around the crystal bowl to keep it from resonating. Sweet chariot! Had Lucifer been doing this every time the door chimes rang?

"Just a minute!" she shouted toward the door. "I'm coming! Don't ring the bell again!" She let go of the bowl and hurried across the long front hall of the rambling, family-sized small-town New England house, but she was too late. The chimes were ringing even as she clutched the doorknob, and when she yanked open the door, her ex-husband was just taking his finger away from the bell.

Grace froze in midgesture. It was a shock. It was more than a shock. Coming as it did on top of the discovery of Lucifer's illicit rapture, it was a double-voltage current that zapped her speechless. She mustered all the breath she had left to utter a single, prayer-felt obscenity.

"Grace," Max said, after a lengthy stretch of disconcerted silence. "I guess I must have surprised you."

"That's one way to put it."

He was freshly shaven, wearing a brand-new, blindingly white T-shirt under a black leather jacket that hung loose on wide shoulders and over a lean, washboard-muscled abdomen. One hand was bandaged across the knuckles, like a prizefighter's. Street brawler's stance, she mused, and cobalt-blue eyes. His gaze flicked toward the half-open door, then fixed steadily on her.

She felt a quiver of panic tickle the back of her throat. Dammit, she'd put in two months of serious, conscientious effort at recovering from Max Hogan. She'd rearranged her life, given up sex, and installed her goldfish in Max's last, bribery-minded peace offering. What kind of a basis was that for social interaction? "What are you doing here, Max?"

He stared at her, not answering, his eyebrows drawn into a frown, while she held the door at half-mast, neither open nor shut, clutching it with both hands.

"You having some trouble with the door?" he asked finally.

Yes, she thought. *It opens. And an ex-husband walks through it.* She didn't quite have the presence of mind to shut it in his face, and by the time the thought occurred to her, he was in, standing in her front hall, looking her over and getting an eyeful of shapeless T-shirt—one of his, in fact—worn jeans, and disheveled hair hanging to her shoulders.

Grace crossed her arms in front of her braless chest and told herself it made no difference one way or the other what she was wearing or what Max thought of it.

To prove it to herself she turned her back on him and led him through the hallway, letting Max trail behind her to the kitchen. If he wanted to talk to her, dammit, he could do so over a cup of hazelnut decaf, in surroundings that didn't include Lucifer, who seemed to have recovered and was again gobbling fish flakes. She didn't want Max to notice Lucifer's high-priced digs, or his unusual enjoyment of them. Knowing Max, he'd make something of it.

She got out a mug from the kitchen cabinet, poured Max a cup of coffee, and handed it to him.

"Thanks."

Grace nodded.

He chose one of the mismatched kitchen chairs they'd picked up at a Saturday-night auction, glancing at it as he pulled it out with his bandaged hand.

She wasn't going to ask him what he'd done to himself, she resolved.

And she wasn't going to point out that the chair he was sitting in was the one with the loose back, the one they'd broken one evening after dinner, when she was on Max's lap. Max had ferried her to the sofa and carried on.

As a matter of fact, that might have been the very night they had . . . unknowingly . . .

Unnerved, Grace plunked her own coffee cup down on the table, an antique Arts-and-Crafts piece with a tendency to rock onto one of its slightly too short legs.

Max rescued his coffee in one practiced gesture, grabbing the mug before it could slide across the canted tabletop, and leaned over to examine the table. "The leg's a little tilted," he said helpfully, glancing back at her. "That's the problem."

"Mm."

"Wouldn't take much to fix it. Glue a piece of dowel on the bottom. A little sandpaper, some varnish, good as new."

"Max," she said, staring at him levelly, "you didn't even know what sandpaper *was* until we got married."

"Yeah, well, I—"

"You thought varnish was the clear stuff in the bottle next to the nail polish."

"That was only the first—"

"When you realized that lawns occasionally needed cutting, I had to take you to the shed and point out the lawn mower before you recognized it."

"Hey, I grew up in a downtown neighborhood. We didn't mow anything in the yard. We just hosed it off."

"I know that!"

"Yeah," he said after a moment. "I guess you do." He studied her, rubbing the edge of his coffee mug with his index finger. "My sister's twins really liked the water guns you gave them for their birthday."

"Oh." Grace sighed, some of her righteous anger deflating. "Did they? They said they did, of course, but I wasn't sure it was the right thing for a birthday present."

"No, it was a great birthday present. Perfect. I wish I'd thought of water guns. Or . . . anything," he added, muttering the last word.

"You mean . . ." Her gaze sharpened, and most of her righteous anger returned in full force. "Oh, Max. Don't tell me you forgot your nephews' birthday!"

"Give me a break, Grace. I've got eleven of them." He paused. "Twelve."

"So you can just forget a couple? You have a good enough supply already? You don't need any more?"

"No! And anyway, I didn't forget. I was just, as my sister pointed out, a little . . . ah . . ." He took a breath, exhaled, and said, without removing his gaze from her face, "You look great, Grace."

She let go of her mug abruptly. The table wobbled

back to its home position, and Max did another rescue-the-coffee move.

"Why are you here, Max?" She hadn't seen him in almost two months—counting down toward official divorce. He'd shown up unannounced, caught her looking like a bag lady, and *admitted* he wasn't responsible enough to be a decent uncle, never mind that he . . .

Never mind.

Max was perusing her face with his soulful blue eyes, saying without words what he'd just told her, and looking mightily like a man whose fondest hope was that she would tell him he looked good too.

Was he crazy?

More to the point, *did* he look good?

A vibrant, quicksilver . . . something passed along all the nerve endings from the back of her neck to the tips of her toes. Grace set her teeth, sat up straighter in her chair, and cleared her throat. "Let's get this over with, Max. State your business."

"What? Like name, rank, and serial number? You got a firing squad waiting out back?"

"I wouldn't shoot you, Max. It's illegal."

The fleeting hint of wounded response in his eyes made her bite her lip, but she didn't take back the remark. She had too much at stake to get into the logistics of shooting Max. Or the reasons for not shooting Max.

"Way harsh, Gracie," he said.

At the use of her nickname, Grace stiffened and glared at him.

"All right," he said. "I'm here strictly on a professional basis, okay? In the interest of your business."

"What interest do you have in my business?"

He gazed at her for another moment, then put his mug back on the table and said carefully, "It's about that Jacob's Ladder bitters flask you were planning to sell."

Her bitters flask? Her appraised-at-twelve-thousand-dollars bitters flask?

"The one you're selling for What's-his-name," Max added.

"What's-his-name? You mean Edmund? Edmund Goodbody?"

"You're on a first-name basis with this guy? Just for selling some bottle?"

"It's a twelve-thousand-dollar bottle."

"I know that. I also know, from doing a little research this morning, that your aunt Lillian's the one who put you on to it."

Grace frowned.

"And the reason that Lillian wanted you to handle this bottle sale might be that this Grubbody guy, it turns out, is the executor of his late uncle's million-dollar estate."

"*Good*body," Grace said. "And his uncle's name was Martin. Edmund's a perfectly logical choice to be executor for Martin Goodbody's estate."

"Uh-huh. He may be perfectly logical, but I don't think that explains Lillian's interest in it. Guess who Martin was married to, as her third husband, before she ditched him to go on to a newer model?"

Grace didn't have to guess. She knew. *Aunt Lillian.* "Aunt Lillian," she said.

"That's right. Martin Goodbody was Lillian's third husband."

"So?"

". . . So?"

"So what does that mean?" Grace asked. "Lillian divorced Martin twenty years ago. She doesn't inherit any of the estate, and I doubt she'd want it anyway. It's all antiques. She just happened to know the family and recommended me for the bottle sale."

"Then why'd she hire me to investigate the bottle?"

Grace banged her mug down on the table again, beating Max's reflexes for once and sloshing hot coffee on his bandaged hand. "You're working for *Lillian*?"

"Jeez, Gracie," he said, transferring his mug and shaking his hand. "I'm just the messenger, for Pete's sake. I'm just telling you something you ought to know."

"What? That Lillian is hatching another plan? Interfering in my life? Being devious and—and *you're* here helping her out! Dammit, did it ever occur to Lillian to butt out of my personal life? Did it ever occur to you, for that matter?"

"No. I thought it was *your* idea."

Grace closed her mouth, momentarily silenced in their mutual standoff.

Max made a futile pass over the table, looking for a dry spot, then gave up and put his mug down in the puddle. "Listen, Gracie, maybe there's more to it than that. I mean, Lillian's had almost two months to come up with a scheme. Why would it take her that long? Someone as calculating as Lillian?"

"Well, I don't know." Grace shrugged. "Maybe . . ." She made a little gesture, feeling the heat of deviousness rise in her own face as she brushed at the wet spot on the table and avoided Max's eyes. "Maybe she just found out . . . something."

"What?"

"I . . . ah . . ." Alarm snaked up into her throat again. Dammit, she should have known she couldn't trust Lillian with any kind of sensitive information!

"About the bottle?" Max asked, conveniently delivering her from a direct answer. "*Is* there something fishy about it, Grace? Is Lillian up to something with this Edmund character?"

"No! Of course not! I wouldn't be selling this flask if I had any doubts about its authenticity. And whatever Lillian's up to, it has nothing to do with Edmund. He's much too nice a man to be cooking something up with my aunt."

"What does that mean—much too nice a man? What is he, a personal friend or something?"

"Yes. In fact, he is."

"*How* personal?"

"That's none of your—"

"The hell it isn't!" Max leaned both hands on the table, which tilted again and spilled a little waterfall of coffee onto the floor.

"We're divorced, Max! Practically."

"That doesn't mean I'm going to sit by here while some lecherous old con artist is trying to run some scam on my wife!"

"He's not lecherous. He's not an old con artist, either. He's very well bred. He has that sort of British boarding school boyish charm, actually."

"Boyish charm? What does that mean?"

"Oh, for heaven's sake, Max, it doesn't mean anything, and it's none of your business anyway, because I'm not your wife!"

"You are too still my wife, Gracie. You've barely even filed for divorce."

"It takes more than a piece of paper to make a marriage, Max. It's not just a written statement. It's not just a casual agreement to live together, either. It's more than fun and games and—and hopping into a hot tub!"

Max stared at her, scowling across the invisible battlement raised by the hot tub Issue—an accusation so fraught with tensions that the moves and countermoves could have been choreographed like a martial arts scene in a Bruce Lee movie, complete with bodies strewn around at the end of it. Max pressed his mouth into a thin, nonargumentative line and, without a word of complaint, moved his foot back from the stream of coffee, which was still dripping off the table.

She wasn't exactly playing fair, Grace admitted to herself, pushing down the guilt trying to niggle its way into her conscience.

The issue wasn't exactly the hot tub.

Or the saleslady in the bikini.

Or even Aunt Lillian's deviousness. It was Grace's own deviousness that was making her feel guilty—and weakening her defenses.

In spite of herself, she got up and reached across the sink for a sponge, which she handed to Max.

He wiped off his shoe, mopped the table, then tossed the sponge into the sink and turned his probing blue gaze back to Grace.

"What if there is something going on here?" he asked finally. "Besides Lillian's usual shenanigans."

"Like what?"

"I don't know. Yet."

Her head shot up. She didn't like the sound of that. "Listen, Max, you can just stop this investigation nonsense right now. And you can tell Lillian she should have hired someone else. Sending you to show up on my doorstep on a Saturday morning was a dead end. Any woman other than Lillian would know that Saturday mornings are for vacuuming the living room, not for receiving visits from ex-husbands."

"I didn't know there was a social convention to this," he muttered.

"There is."

"Well, pardon me if I got in the way of your vacuum cleaner, but I have a feeling there's something going on here that somebody needs to get to the bottom of."

"What?"

"I'm not sure. But I have an instinct about this case."

"Oh?" She pushed herself back from the table. "You have an instinct? I'm supposed to drop my biggest sales opportunity in months because you have an instinct that needs to be indulged?"

Max's reaction was silent, sexy, and completely visceral. He blinked. Just one flicker of the baby blues, but it immediately brought to mind half a dozen times when Grace had dropped her work to indulge one of Max's instincts. Not to mention what he'd dropped: clients, phone calls, pants.

On more than one occasion when they'd snatched an hour to meet at home for lunch, they'd left paths of strewn clothes through the hall, up the stairs, flung over the antique bedposts. There were still smudged spots on the ancient Oriental where Max had carried her, dripping because she'd followed him out into the rain to kiss him good-bye. He'd decided his investigation could wait another half hour, and Grace had left her last can of antique crackle glaze hardening on the back porch while she and Max added a real-life layer of "distressed patina" to the sleigh-back sofa in the front room.

She felt a flush spread across her face. Her heart was beating as if they were about to have another memorable encounter involving Max's naked chest under her cheek, Max holding her, his hands on her thighs, guiding her . . .

"No," she said, her voice a little thin. "No. Absolutely not. No distressed sofas, no investigations, no nothing! I want you out of here. Now."

"Distressed sofas?"

She pushed her chair back, stood, and pointed toward the door. "Out, Hogan! You know the meaning of the word?"

"Yeah." He stood up. "Thanks to you, I do."

She let that one go and followed him to the front room, fuming.

Max, evidently, was doing some fuming of his own.

He stopped in front of Lucifer, stared for a disbelieving moment, then gave her a look that could have distressed a sofa with no help at all. "I see you found a use for the crystal punch bowl I gave you, Gracie."

"This is the default use," she snapped back. "My first idea was to use it for target practice, but I'm a lousy shot."

"Thank God for small favors." He leaned over, examined the bowl, and snapped his middle finger against the rim. The crystal chimed out in perfect, sympathetic resonance. Lucifer stopped feeding, shivered all over, and went into spasm. "Hey!" Max muttered. "What's with the fish?"

"Dammit!" Grace exploded, diving for the bowl. "You leave my fish alone!"

Max caught her wrists just as she wrapped her hands around the crystal and pulled her away from the bowl. Yanking her against his body, he pinned her by crossing her arms over her chest and dragged her back from the hall table.

"Max!" she exclaimed, her voice panic-stricken. "What do you think you're doing?"

"It's called self-protection, babe! I'm not about to get beaned with my own punch bowl!"

"I wasn't going to hit you with it!"

"You weren't?"

"You just can't help yourself, can you? If there's any possibility for transcendent sex, you just have to walk up to it and snap your finger against it."

There was a short pause, then Max asked, his tone suspicious, "Are you talking about the fish?"

Was she talking about the fish? What kind of an innuendo-edged question was that? Of course she was talking about the fish! What else would she be talking about?

Unfortunately, what else she might be talking about was all too obvious, with her inadequately covered backside pressed against the front of Max's jeans. The hollows and hillocks of Max fit with familiar, graphic suggestion into the hillocks and hollows of Grace. It had happened before. Often. A sweet, sensual introduction to sweet, soul-shattering sex. Grace knew how the process worked. Her runaway imagination had no trouble conjuring up images that weakened her knees.

Max knew how the process worked too. If she had any doubt about that, she knew she could forget it when his hold on her wrists gentled, just enough to suggest coaxing rather than coercing, and his head tipped down to hers until the side of his face brushed her hair. "Gracie," he murmured, "I don't really have any sexual interest in your fish." His voice got a little lower, a little more sensual. "Or in anyone other than my wife. I never did. I can swear to that, Gracie. If you want me to prove it, I'll be more than happy to give you proof."

"Proof?" she murmured. The word came out halfway between a sigh and a moan. There was something wrong with her breathing. Something had gone completely awry with her thought processes too. The heat of Max's body seeping into hers, the touch of his big, callused hands on the sensitive skin of her wrists was so mesmerizing, it defied any attempts at sensible reasoning. And the soft, rushed cadence of his breath against her skin elicited an answering, breathless cadence of her own.

Seductive warmth poured through her body like the golden sun of April after a long, cold winter. Max hadn't pushed the issue of whether she was still his wife. Not in words. But he was pushing it now, and every insinuation carried layers of remembered emotion—tender yearnings and murmured words and the warm trust of lovers whose hearts were synchronized. Things she'd missed, moments she longed for in the small hours of the night when she lay awake, alone.

His lips touched the edge of her ear, and his breath stirred against the side of her neck. "Don't throw me out again, Gracie."

Throw him out? Was she crazy? Grace wondered, the question swimming up through a sensual haze. *Had* she been crazy? Were their differences really irreconcilable? Responsibility, reality, redecorating the nursery—what did all that matter when measured against this transcendent pulse of passion rushing through her veins, urging her to surrender to something so shattering it would make her feel like . . . Lucifer?

Lucifer. In the punch bowl. She gave the fish a guilty glance. He seemed to have survived the last bout of ecstasy, gobbled up the few remaining fish flakes, and was cruising the water dejectedly, looking a little desperate for another fix.

Grace knew how he felt. You could get hooked on that kind of ecstasy. You could become a creature of pure sensuality, especially if after weeks of deprivation your ex-husband was doing something to your neck with his mouth, whispering sweet nothings in your ear, suggesting things that made your stomach flutter and your breathing erratic. She felt the beginnings of a delicate shudder, a little like Lucifer's, after her ex-husband had snapped his finger against the fishbowl.

Her ex-husband. *Ex-husband.*

Good heavens, what was she doing? Standing in her front hallway, being seduced by her ex-husband? She was worse than Lucifer. She was acting like Lillian.

She wiggled against Max, trying to get away, and in the process, raising hillocks she was entirely too aware of.

"Forget it, Max," she said, her voice still breathless but at least, now, connected to her brain. "And let me go, while you're at it. I'm not going to use the punch bowl as a weapon. I wouldn't do that to my fish!"

He let go of her, reluctantly, taking his time about stepping away from her body, holding her wrists until the last moment.

She yanked her hands back, rubbing her wrists more emphatically than necessary to disguise the flush of inappropriate response in her cheeks. "Divorce is not a contact sport, Max, in case you haven't read the small print."

"What small print?"

"The small print that says I'm not interested in continuing this relationship on an intimate level."

He slid his hands into his pockets, tipped his head back, and gave her a long, evaluative look, processing the data he was receiving but apparently not getting anywhere in figuring out how it was supposed to make sense. "You know, I'm an enlightened, late-twentieth-century male, Grace."

"Congratulations."

"So when you tell me to let go of you, I'm going to take you at your word. But I've got to say, Grace, that statement about how you're not interested in anything intimate is really kind of questionable when measured up against the physical evidence."

"I'd like your physical evidence out of my house, Max, and you can have that in writing. In a divorce decree."

"Yeah? Well, let me tell you something, Gracie. That's just the small print."

She stalked past him, pulled open the front door, and invited him out. "I'm in favor of the small print, Max." She slammed the door on him, but it was about ten seconds too late to cut off her ex-husband's insouciant grin and unanswerable last word.

"Is that a fact?" he said.

TWO

"What do you mean, he's already come and *gone*?" Aunt Lillian demanded over the phone. "Where did he go?"

"I don't—"

"Out for champagne?" Lillian cut in. "To buy cigars? Flowers? To the jeweler's?"

Grace sighed, caught yet again between exasperation and rueful laughter at Lillian's implacable belief in her own version of Grace's life.

"Chenet's or Shraft Diamond, I wonder," Lillian mused. "I hope Chenet's. They have some lovely—"

"No, Aunt Lillian. Not Chenet's. He went home."

"Home?" Lillian was outraged. "*Home?* Without even . . ." Her aunt gasped as reality flew in the face of her cherished imaginative scenario. "Oh, my God," she concluded. "I know what this means. You didn't *tell* him."

Grace's half-smile faded. She slid her hand down

the front of her body until it pressed against her stomach, then drew in a breath through her teeth. "No, I didn't. I've made my decision on that, Aunt Lillian. Sending Max over here on a bogus investigation of my bitters flask isn't going to change anything."

"But why *not*? When I gave you such a *perfect* opportunity?"

"I told you, Aunt Lillian, that I didn't intend—"

"Grace, my *dear*." Aunt Lillian sighed deeply. "When did you develop this belated aptitude for subterfuge and deceit?"

"I haven't developed any—"

"I mean, *really*. All the years when it might have been useful, you couldn't tell the tiniest little fib to save your life. Or mine," she added in a rare correction toward honesty. "And now here you are, lying to poor *clueless* Max about the fact that he's already, unbeknownst to *him*, about to become the father of my grandchild!"

The statement was a typical Lillianesque stretching of the truth. Ten years earlier Aunt Lillian had taken Grace in while Grace's parents were jet-hopping around Asia looking at new import-business opportunities and sending an occasional postcard home.

Aunt Lillian had taken to surrogate parenting with energy and verve. She'd pulled strings to have Grace accepted early to an art-oriented Boston college within commuting distance of their exurban town, then enrolled along with her as a nontraditional student. Grace had studied art history and graduated magna cum laude. Lillian had dabbled in sculpture and painting and had had a notable affair with one of Grace's professors. Grace had made a few friends and settled into college life. Lillian had swept them all off to Italy and rented a sleek, modern villa from an Italian politician, who had turned out to be a marvelous tour guide, if you ignored the one or two little incidents when the mob was after him. Grace had discovered Mozart in a Music 101 course. Lillian had introduced her to grunge rock, performed live in a Boston harborside atmosphere that had made Grace's eyes water.

Lillian had also introduced her to Max—a spectacularly successful matchmaking effort that in Lillian's mind wiped out all her previously lukewarm successes at livening up Grace's life.

There'd never been any doubt about it, Grace admitted. Max could sizzle her bacon in half a sentence or with one across-the-room look. She and Max had made each other breathless the day they met, and after a year of marriage they'd still been too breathless for the kind of sober conversation Grace had tried to have.

"If Max is clueless," Grace said levelly, "it's because he wants to be."

"No it isn't. It's because you haven't *told* him!"

Grace sagged against the counter, her shoulders slumped. "It's not that I haven't tried, Aunt Lillian. I *tried* mentioning it two months ago in every possible way it could be done. I brought up the subject of *family* in so many convoluted conversations, even I couldn't figure out what I was talking about. Max Hogan just didn't want to hear it."

"Sometimes men can be a little *slow*, Grace."

"Slow?" She pushed herself away from the counter and straightened her shoulders. "No, Aunt Lillian. I don't think *slow* is the word. The day I decided I was going to tell him anyway, and he was going to have to listen up, I came home and discovered he'd spent *all* our savings, which we could have used to put in a nursery, on a *hot tub*. And he was in it. With the saleslady!"

"Max does have that effect on some women."

"Murderous rage?"

"Mm," Lillian said, a noncommittal, musical hum. "But I was thinking of other, more sensual—"

"No, he doesn't."

"Oh, my," Lillian purred, picking up on the nuances. "I guess he didn't waste any time, did he?"

Grace grimaced at the phone in her hand. How was she supposed to answer that? Not that it mattered. Aunt Lillian had a sixth sense for picking up sexual sparks between any two people, anywhere, under any circumstances.

"No, Aunt Lillian," Grace said. "Max doesn't ever waste any time."

"Well, then?" Lillian asked, ignoring the irony in Grace's edgy comment.

"Well, then, nothing. I didn't tell him because he doesn't really want to know. He just isn't . . . ready, Aunt Lillian! He's not going to trade in his Mustang convertible for a family van, or a—a redecorating job on this house! Family activity wasn't what he had in mind when he bought us that hot tub for our anniversary."

She pressed her hand harder against her still-flat

stomach, then lifted her chin and clenched her jaw tightly enough to feel it in her back teeth. It hurt—Max's attitude. But the truth was the truth. "I have some pride, Aunt Lillian. Max Hogan doesn't want responsibility, parenthood, and a pregnant wife, and I'm not going to coerce him into it."

She'd reduced her aunt to silence, Grace realized when no answer was forthcoming over the phone. Finally Lillian uttered a puzzled and sincere, "Why not?"

"Because . . . because . . ." Grace's voice trailed off into a frustrated laugh. Lillian was incapable of understanding why any woman wouldn't coerce a man into whatever she could dream up, if she could get away with it. "Because I don't *want* a husband who considers me . . . us . . . a drag on his lifestyle."

"Mm," Lillian said, another musical hum that indicated the conversation was moving beyond her sphere of interest. "Actually, dear, it's *your* lifestyle I'm concerned about."

"My lifestyle?"

"Max was so good for you, Grace. Helping you loosen up a bit. Lose a few inhibitions. En*joy* life. You've gotten so *serious*. So . . . *conservative*."

Grace's mouth quirked up at one corner. Aunt Lillian's idea of conservative was listening to rock music without tearing off one's outer layer of clothes.

"And you do have a tendency in that direction, darling," Lillian went on, "if you don't mind my saying so."

"Aunt Lillian," she burst out, exasperated. "I'm going to be a parent. That's—" A tiny, icy thread of alarm scurried down her spine. *That's unexpected. Overwhelming. Terrifying.* "That's serious," she said.

"Oh, *no*, not at all, darling! It's a marvelous, *freeing* experience. Why, having you move in as my surrogate daughter was nothing but *fun!*"

Grace covered her eyes with one hand and suppressed the comment that it hadn't, exactly, been *nothing but fun*, not from Grace's point of view. She loved her aunt, and she wasn't unappreciative of all that Lillian had done for her, but she'd often ended up feeling more like a survivor than a cherished daughter.

"Why, remember that trip to Coney Island, Grace? I never would have thought of riding that roller coaster if I hadn't been entertaining you. Having a child keeps you *young*. That young Cyclone operator took us for sisters. Well, we do look so much alike, you know, it's uncanny."

"Aunt Lillian, I was paralyzed with fear on that roller coaster!"

"Oh, you were a little reluctant at first, but then it was *wonderful*." As usual, Lillian's blithe confidence was unshaken. "And poor Max is being *left out* of all that!"

Grace sighed. Maybe she would have liked to be left off this emotional roller coaster, herself. "I'll deal with Max's parental rights after the divorce, Aunt Lillian. Right now I just can't get into that kind of emotional issue with him. It's too . . ." Anxiety attacked her again. Grace ignored it. "Too emotional. The marriage is over. That's all I can handle right now. And anyway, nothing he or I could say would change that."

"Mm. Maybe he should have gone with a gift of jewelry instead of that crystal bowl . . ."

"No, Aunt Lillian. He definitely should not have gone with jewelry. He shouldn't have gone with crystal, either. I didn't want gifts."

"Mm. You know, I must say, Grace, if Max Hogan showed up on *my* doorstep with a Waterford crystal punch bowl, I'd take it."

That was the problem, Grace thought. Aunt Lillian would. Her aunt had been married and divorced often enough to make it a formal field of study, based on something Lillian called "romantic sparks," which were all that really counted. Responsibility, conservatism, and mowing the lawn were dismissible traits. Stray transgressions on the part of husbands were handled with expensive gifts.

"Aunt Lillian? Why are you sending Max over here on this phony investigation now? You've known for more than a month that I was pregnant. What else is going on that I should know about?"

"Mm. I really must go, darling. I have an appointment for a facial. *Do* think about what I've said, won't you?"

The phone clicked off as Lillian hung up, having managed to evade, as usual, all uncomfortable questions from her niece or her conscience.

Grace stared out toward the front room, her jaw tightening again, then pushed herself away from the counter and marched out there.

A silver-footed Waterford crystal punch bowl containing two gallons of water and one goldfish was a little more than Grace could comfortably handle, but she managed to get it to the kitchen counter, where she poured the contents, including Lucifer, into his old aquarium.

"It's for your own good, Lucifer," she told him. "It's over, you understand? Kaput. Finis. No more punch bowl ecstasy. No more physical stuff at all, for either one of us. That's final."

Lucifer stared back at her, looking troubled.

"Don't look at me like that," Grace said.

His expression didn't change by so much as a fish fin.

"There are no more romantic sparks between me and Max!"

Lucifer didn't deign to comment, but when she glanced toward him again he didn't appear sympathetic. In fact, he was waving his gill fins forlornly, as if he were hearing her absolute resolutions but seeing deficiencies of character he couldn't believe, and it saddened him, just saddened him.

Grace looked away, then let out a long sigh.

But she couldn't quite resist leaning over and giving the punch bowl a little ping.

"The way I see it," Ernie said an hour later, around a mouthful of the chocolate-covered doughnut with which Max had bribed him, "you blew it. You should have let her bean you with the punch bowl."

"What are you talking about? She could've knocked me senseless."

"Yeah. She would've felt guilty as hell."

"That's great, Ernie. My ex-wife feels guilty and I feel unconscious."

Ernie wiped a dab of chocolate off the corner of his mouth. "Tell you the truth, Max, that's not a whole lot different than what the two of you have been ever since you broke up."

"Huh?"

"Hey, you could have woken up with your head in her lap, those big brown eyes looking down on you, those soft little hands stroking your forehead . . ."

Max's chair legs hit the floor, shaking him up but not coming close to matching the jolt he felt at imagining Grace leaning over him, her unbound breasts a breath away from his mouth, her soft eyes gazing down at him fondly, a little guiltily maybe, wanting to make it up to him.

Max pressed his hand to his chest, breathing hard, trying to throttle that pesky sprig of hope that seemed to be getting him lately.

Ernie frowned, then leaned forward to get a better look at Max. "You okay, buddy?"

"A few stray regrets," Max told him. "Or else I'm having a heart attack."

"I'd go with the regrets," Ernie said.

Not if he'd felt them, he wouldn't, Max decided. What the hell was the matter with him? He'd been fine yesterday. A few disconcertingly vivid fantasies about Grace, maybe. A minor problem getting back into circulation. A lingering obsession or two. The point was, he'd gotten over her.

Then Lillian had conned him into this cockamamy investigation and, what was more inexplicable, he'd let himself be conned. He must be nuts.

That was it. He'd lost all contact with reality, as evidenced by the fact that for a moment there he'd been considering the benefits of being knocked into emergency room status by a punch bowl he'd paid for himself.

"Have a doughnut," Ernie offered. "And lay off the caffeinated coffee."

"I don't have a caffeine problem, Ernie. I have a death wish."

"I guess you'd qualify on that point, judging from the jobs you've been taking lately."

Max grunted. "Is that fax in yet?" It was his only hope for sanity. Get the information from the police computer files, satisfy himself that there were no estate law glitches that could get Grace into trouble, then drop the whole idea and distract himself with a couple of high-action cases, preferably involving a few scrapes with death. In a near-death situation, he could go fifteen minutes at a time without thinking of Grace.

"What's your hurry?" Ernie asked. "Look at it this way: No one's tried to knife you in at least an hour. Your occupational safety is way up for the day."

Up from what? Max wondered. Encountering his ex-wife? Being semipermanently crippled from the stress on his gonads? Having his mental health pulped and rerolled?

"You tell Lillian about the goldfish going into spasms?" Ernie asked.

"No."

"Why not?"

Max considered the question. "Lillian's not into religious experiences, I don't think."

"You think it was religious?"

"Nirvana for one."

"As opposed to *Nirvana for two*?"

Max opened his mouth to ask what the hell Ernie meant by that, then shut it as a little sound wafted through the back of his mind. The one Grace had made when he'd whispered in her ear. That low, wordless, soulful sigh that was, sometimes, the prelude to what he'd have to describe as—

The fax machine on the next desk whirred.

"Hey—here we go." Ernie leaned across to get the fax.

"So what's the story?"

"Hm. Doesn't look like much. Martin Goodbody died two months ago. He left a will, duly probated. Edmund Goodbody, his nephew, is the executor."

"I knew that."

Ernie gave him a look.

"Edmund's the bottle salesman," Max said. "The guy with the bitters flask."

"The one Lillian thinks is stolen?"

"It's not stolen," Max said gloomily. "Edmund's a *very nice* man with boyish charm."

"Then why'd you ask me to raid the police files?"

"What else is on there?"

Ernie went back to the fax. "Martin's estate goes half to his sister, Edmund's mother, Marian Goodbody—she kept her maiden name. Apparently her husband didn't mind, and if he did, it's too late to protest. He died ten years ago. And the other half goes to his sister-in-law, Eloise Goodbody, who was married to Martin's older brother, also dead."

"The men in the family don't seem to last long, do they?"

"Except for Edmund."

Max grunted, aware of a small hope that Edmund might meet the same male Goodbody fate. Either that or lose all his boyish charm before he spoke to Grace again.

"Just the two of them—Marian and the sister-in-law, Eloise—get the estate," Ernie said.

"Nothing for Lillian, huh?"

"Nope. Doesn't seem to be. Everything's supposed to be auctioned off, the proceeds split down the middle. Specific instructions. Apparently he didn't trust Marian and Eloise to divvy things up on their own. That must be why he named Edmund as executor."

"And no mention of his ex-wife Lillian?"

"Nope. There's a note here—police record. Martin's house was broken into ten years ago. Seems like a painting was stolen. Never recovered."

"That's all you have?"

Ernie flipped to the second page of the fax. "Well, lookit this. There is something else. A codicil. About Edmund."

"What? Let me see that."

"He gets an inheritance, once the estate is disposed of to Martin's specifications."

"What kind of inheritance?"

"Hundred thou. There's a note here that Martin has the utmost faith in Edmund's judgment, discretion, and family loyalty."

Max stood up and snatched the paper out of Ernie's hands. "What's that mean? Judgment, family loyalty?"

"Sounds like he's a solid citizen, upright member of the community, and about to get a pretty good nest egg too."

"So what's that make him? Bachelor of the year?"

Ernie shrugged. "With that kind of money, I'd say yeah."

"So what's he gonna do, just pick some woman he's maybe working with and propose to her?" Max was outraged.

"Sounds like he might have to beat them off, tell you the truth." Ernie's cheerful tone came close to insufferable.

"Hey," the officer next to Ernie said, as Max stormed out of the station house. "Where's that man going with that fax? He got some reason to be walking out of here with police information?"

"Yeah," Ernie said. "Something to do with a religious experience."

By twelve-thirty on Saturday, Grace Hogan was sitting at a little round table in the Blue Moon, across the street from Max's office. She had her shoes off, her toes curled around the chair rail, and her elbows propped beside her plate as she bit into a Moonburger special with onions and french fries.

She was starving. She'd spent the last hour and a half of the morning looking for Max, determined she was going to find him and call him off, before he showed up on her doorstep again, unannounced, catching her with her guard down. His smug, knowing *Is that a fact?* exit had left her edgy and unsettled.

Unfortunately, her determined, take-charge errand had been undermined by acute hunger pangs. She took another big bite of hamburger, wolfing it down exactly the way Lucifer had attacked his fish flakes in postrapturous frenzy.

The comparison wasn't lost on her.

She ought to send Max a bill for the lunch, including dessert.

As soon as she found him.

"Grace? Are you looking for me?"

Startled, she jerked the hamburger away from her mouth, onions sliding out of the roll onto her fingers, and twisted her head around to look at him. Damn him, he'd done it again, caught her off guard, with her hands around a hamburger which, though she wasn't about to admit it, was evidence of just what kind of effect he had on her.

"No," she said irritably, putting down the sandwich and reaching for her napkin. "I was looking for you earlier. What I'm doing now is eating lunch."

"Sorry I'm late," he said dryly. He walked around the table and pulled out the other chair, raising an eyebrow at her.

"By all means, sit down."

"Thanks."

"How did you track me down here, anyway? I was looking for *you*, for Pete's sake."

"Yeah, I know. Lillian told me."

"She did?" She lowered her napkin to her lap, assessing the situation.

"So?" Max said. "Here I am."

Here he was. Grace squashed her napkin into a little soggy ball. He said it the way he'd announce the delivery of a bridal shower cake stuffed with a male stripper. And guess who was doing the sexy honors?

"You're fired, Max," she said, taking a certain amount of satisfaction in it.

"What?"

"From the case. Lillian's calling it off. Your services are no longer needed. So that's that."

He didn't look as if that was that. He had that dangerous, iron-simmering-in-the-forge look that wasn't described by "that's that."

Grace felt another shot of bioelectrical current, like a tiny, preliminary warning of one of Lucifer's rapture spasms. She picked up her hamburger, coaxing stray onions back into place with one finger and once again avoiding Max's gaze. God, she was hungry.

"Lillian's backing off?" he asked.

"I talked to her this morning," Grace said, around a bite of Moonburger. "After you left. I told her she had no business butting into my life, and she agreed she was completely in the wrong."

"*Lillian?*"

"Well . . ." Grace's recently acquired aptitude for deception deserted her, inconveniently. "Well, not in so many words," she hedged. Not in any words, actually.

There was silence from across the table.

"The point is, the investigation is off." Grace took a nervous bite of her hamburger, then chased it with a french fry.

"Gracie," Max said, "has it been a long time since you've eaten?"

She glared at him. "Did I ask you to join me here?"

"No."

"Did I invite you to lunch?"

"No."

"Did I even indicate that I wanted to see you again, ever?"

"I thought you wanted to tell me I was fired."

"You're fired. Okay?"

"Okay," he shot back, scowling.

He didn't get up and leave.

Grace took another bite.

"You meeting a client?" Max asked.

It was the logical conclusion. She was wearing her best suit, a blue linen ensemble she'd donned to make up for the sweatshirt and no underwear she'd had on earlier, and she was gobbling her lunch with linen-threatening abandon. "No," she said, reluctantly disclaiming the obvious excuse for dressing up. "My current client, as it happens, is out of town."

"The bottle guy? I know."

"You *know*? What do you mean, you know? What have you been doing—tailing him too?"

"Electronically speaking. Why? Is there anything about him I should know? Besides his boyish charm?"

"Of course not! Edmund is an honest citizen."

'Not to mention rich."

"Rich?"

"Grace, this Edmund character—he gets a cut of the inheritance. A big cut."

"Oh."

"You telling me you didn't know that?"

"I knew that. He's the executor, after all. That's a lot of work. He deserves some compensation. But what has that got to—"

"You mean he *told* you about it?"

Grace frowned, the burger halfway to her mouth. "Yes."

"Oh, really? I suppose he just casually mentioned it, huh? Like, 'Oh, by the way, I'm going to have a hundred thou when this is all through'—nice little nest egg, don't you think?"

She gave him a blank look.

"He did, didn't he?" Max added, outraged.

"Well, yes, he did, but I don't understand—"

"He *did*? Oh, jeez. I might have known that." Max swiped a hand across his forehead in derision, then, for good measure, let out a snort of contempt. "This guy's on the make, Gracie!"

"What?"

"And you don't even know it!"

"That's ridiculous."

Max glowered at her, but Grace's animosity was temporarily forgotten as she considered that Max had completely lost his grip on reality. Max was threatened by *Edmund*? The idea was . . .

"That's ridiculous," she said again. "And anyway . . ."

"Anyway, what?"

". . . Nothing." She clutched her hamburger.

"No, what? What were you going to say?"

"Max . . ."

"You were going to say you're still married, right? To me. You were going to say we're not divorced yet, weren't you?"

"That's—" She took a breath. *That's true*, her conscience prompted. She ignored it. "Lots of people get divorced, Max. Perfectly nice people. Often it's for the best."

Max didn't move, she could swear he didn't, but something in his face gave her the distinct impression of a flinch, as if she'd hit him.

"Like when?" he asked, barely moving his mouth to get the words out. "Like when, exactly, is it for the best?"

Grace found she was suddenly having trouble getting words out, herself. All the logical, coherent reasons for divorcing Max that came so readily to mind when she was talking to Lucifer seemed to get stuck in a corner of her brain when she was actually facing him, seeing the expression on his face. "Like . . . when two people shouldn't have gotten married in the first place," she managed to say, snagged, badly, on that look.

"Shouldn't have gotten married in the *first* place?"

"When they don't have anything in common. When—"

"Anything in *common*? What's that supposed to mean? Like what? They don't . . ." He gestured, searching for his argument. "Both wear the same T-shirts? Both read the same paper, both read the same comics first? They don't both like Chinese take-out in bed? Or all the rest of it?"

He had found his voice, but it was coming from somewhere deeper than his larynx, a rough, low growl that crept up the back of her spine and set off nerve endings all along its way. Grace put her Moonburger down, clutched her napkin, and tried to get her lungs working on full capacity and her pulse beating in some kind of normal rhythm.

"They don't make sparks together?" he went on. "Sparks, hell. They don't threaten to burn the whole damn neighborhood down when they get it on?" His gaze locked with hers. "When they don't spend every morning daydreaming about the night before, every afternoon waiting for the night to come? Is that when, Gracie?"

"No. Yes. *No.* I don't want to talk about it. I'm just not—"

"Interested?" he finished, giving the word innuendos that could have made her punch bowl resonate. "Because I have to tell you, Gracie, you were interested this morning."

"I was not."

"No? I know what you look like when you're interested. I ought to know, the times we *got* interested."

"Max . . ."

"You want the details? Your face flushes, and your eyes have a little flicker in them, and you're breathing a little faster than normal, and you start wiggling your ankle, in that sexy way you have, and then—"

"Stop that." She sat up straighter and put both feet flat on the floor, where nothing was wiggling. She wasn't breathing faster. Not noticeably, anyway. And her face wasn't warm. And her eyes were not flickering. Her throat hadn't gone dry, either, and she didn't feel a half-audible moan gathering in her chest. He'd missed those last two signs.

She took another bite of her burger and added two or three french fries and a pickle.

"Don't let me stop you from enjoying your lunch," he said, sounding a little wounded.

"Oh, for Pete's sake." She stopped eating, with an effort, and sighed.

Max was watching her with a mixture of rejected machismo and incredulity, as if he couldn't believe she'd just listened to his description of their sex life and hadn't dropped her hamburger and prepared to take up exactly where they'd left off two months ago.

Or two hours ago, to get technical.

Five minutes ago, if he was talking about pure mental imagery.

Sweet chariot, what was the matter with her? Why didn't she *care* about his rejected machismo?

"Aren't you going to order?" she asked finally.

"Not right now."

She frowned. "You're not hungry?"

"No. But go ahead. Stave off starvation for the both of us."

She took another bite, but it was a distracted action as she contemplated the comment: both of us. She was, in fact, eating for two. She was, if the truth be told, carrying her ex-husband's baby. She was, actually, pregnant.

And she was, in court-of-law technicality, keeping that fact from her husband.

He was staring at her, his blue eyes slightly accusing and looking like he . . . cared.

"Have you lost weight?" she asked him.

"I don't know."

"You have, haven't you?"

"I don't know, maybe."

He shrugged, managing to look more wounded, as if he couldn't be bothered keeping up his weight since she'd thrown him out.

"What did you do to your hand?" she asked.

He turned his wrist to glance at the bandage covering all four knuckles of his right hand. "You mean before I burned it with hot coffee?"

"Yes, well . . ."

"Nothing serious. I cut myself."

"On the job?"

"Yeah."

She put her hamburger down again. Her appetite had disappeared, for some reason. "What kind of job?"

Max was looking puzzled once more. "Have you been talking to Ernie?"

"No. What's Ernie got to do with your hand?"

"Just something he's always telling me."

Grace didn't say anything. The conversation seemed to have wandered onto dangerous ground. She was feeling a poignant tug at her emotions that went below, beneath, beyond any physical pull that Max still had over her.

"Grace?" he asked, after a long pause. "Do you feel . . . guilty?"

"*Guilty?*"

She didn't feel guilty. She was affronted that he should ask. But, annoyingly, her voice squeaked with guilt, and a hot flush was rising up from her collar. "No, I don't feel guilty! You're the one who was in the hot tub with the bimbo. Just who has Ernie been talking to? Lillian?"

"No, although I get the feeling he'd like to."

"Fine. Just tell him to leave me out of his plans."

Max shut his mouth on his next comment, choosing instead to study her for clues.

She gave him one, fidgeting with her fork, a little ashamed of herself. The bimbo in the hot tub was a sideswipe, not the real issue, which was that Grace was the one who had thrown Max out, initiated the divorce, ended a marriage she'd promised to honor until death.

Max's gaze had taken on a quality of revelation that she didn't like at all. "You do feel guilty," he said reflectively, his frown clearing. "Ernie was right."

"About what? You're completely crazy, Max. And

Ernie is wrong. Unless he was talking about you. You're the one who should feel guilty!"

"No, I'm the one who's unconscious."

"What?"

His mouth turned up at the corners, almost smiling. It was a smug masculine smirk, like he'd just figured the goods on her and any moment now she'd be his for the taking. "It's true, isn't it?" he said. "You *have* missed me."

She let out a disgusted breath, crossed her arms in front of her, and sat back in her chair.

Max snagged a french fry from her plate and wolfed it down with every evidence of satisfaction.

THREE

"Eloise? It's Lillian. Is this phone tapped?"

Eloise Goodbody, sister-in-law to the late Martin Goodbody, snorted. "We haven't even committed the crime yet, Lillian. Why would the phone be tapped?"

"God knows, Eloise. It's your phone."

"Yes, but it's in my cleaning lady's name. A little arrangement we have."

The receiver crackled with restrained commentary. "I won't ask," Lillian said.

"I thought Tuesday morning."

"*Tuesday?* Why do we have to wait until Tuesday? I mean, as long as we've decided, why don't we just go *ahead*?"

"No, it's Tuesday. Unless my arthritis kicks up. You know what it's like trying to use those lock picks when your arthritis is kicking up?"

"Well, for heaven's sake, Eloise, just take a couple of aspirin."

"Guess I'll have to. You can't possibly do the locks. Takes years of practice."

"I've had *plenty* of practice! Just not in picking locks."

Eloise snorted again.

"What about the car?" Lillian asked.

"My cleaning lady's getting us a van. She'll leave it in the garage Monday night, late. The keys will be under the mat. Can you drive a stick shift?"

"As long as it has four wheels."

"Oh, it will have at least that," Eloise said.

The comment gave Lillian pause. "I'm not lifting anything heavier than an end table," she said.

"Well, don't expect me to do it, with my back."

"I don't expect *anyone* to do it. We have a *plan*, Eloise. No last-minute improvisation. Unless I think of something."

"My attitude exactly."

"Of course, anything could happen between now and Tuesday."

Eloise sighed. "My cleaning lady will come and get the van when we're through with it."

"Does she do windows too?"

"Oh, no. Hasn't for years."

"I didn't think so."

"Well, then, that should cover it," Eloise said.

"I certainly hope so. God, I hope we don't get caught at this. It would be hard to explain."

"Well," Eloise agreed, "you'd need a very sympathetic police officer."

The line hummed for a thoughtful moment.

"You would," Lillian said. "Wouldn't you?"

"It's busy." Grace put down the phone, leaned back in the swivel chair behind the desk, and glanced at Max. The glance was a little wary, Max noted.

He'd talked her into walking over to his office to call Lillian and report his official firing, but she didn't look especially as if she wanted to be there.

"You can wait a few minutes and try her again," he said.

"I will. I'm not changing my mind on this, Max. You *are* fired."

He rubbed the back of his neck. "I'm fired, yeah. I got that."

"It's not personal."

"Right. Impersonal firing. My favorite way to get canned."

She sighed, and crossed her arms in front of her, then crossed her legs as well. Making a point, Max figured. His glance fell to the suggestive stretch of thigh visible below her hiked-up hem. She yanked her skirt down to her knee and crossed her arms again.

"So," he said, leaping onto a neutral topic, "how's the business going?"

She gave him a level glance. "If I get a good price on this bottle flask, and if I land the appraisal for the Goodbody estate, business will be fine."

Max frowned at her. Was she trying to say something with that *if* part? Grace's antiques-consulting

business had never even had a slump. Both the Associated Auctioneers' cooperative she worked with and the
private clients who contacted her for buying or selling
thought she was the cat's meow in antiques. She *was*
good at it. Probably some kind of reaction to living with
Lillian, Max had always thought. Grace had emerged
from her Lillian-influenced formative years with an in-
clination toward permanence, tradition, and anything
old.

Max's frown deepened. Was Edmund older than he
was? Was Grace going to trade him in for an older
model? One with more patina?

"Last I heard," he said, "your business was fine,
anyway. Now you're telling me you just have to have
this estate? You're going to go under if you don't get
it?"

"I didn't say I was going *under*. I just want to estab-
lish a secure base for . . . the future."

"For the future?"

"Anyway, if you know my business is doing fine,
why'd you ask? How *do* you know?"

"I asked your lawyer."

"You asked my—"

"Hey." Max held up both hands, indicating un-
blamable intent. "He called me."

"Why?"

"Some forms or something."

"Why didn't he call *your* lawyer?"

"Probably because I don't have one."

Grace stared at him. "Max. You need a lawyer."

"What for?"

"To protect your interests in the . . . legal action."

"From you?" he said, keeping the question innocent. "You already threw me out, Gracie. That *was* my interest in the legal action."

Her arms uncrossed a little, and her gaze faltered, the expression in her brown eyes flickering with . . . guilt, Max decided, impressed with his own perception. Definitely guilt. Ernie had been right.

Ernie had been right about her eyes, too, as long as he was noticing. Soft, dark, expressive. Wide with understanding when he'd had a rough day. Sparked with devilment when she teased him. And then they'd get even darker when he took her up on the invitation, when she made that little sound in the back of her throat . . .

"Max?" She was looking wary again. "Are you okay?"

"What? You mean apart from the . . . ah, legal action?"

Her foot started to wiggle. "I didn't *throw* you out, Max. You make it sound as if you were sleeping in the street or something."

"Well, I had my convertible. It leaks a little when it rains, but—"

"And whose fault is that? Of course it leaks in the rain. A seventeen-year-old Mustang is going to leak in the rain. Why didn't you buy yourself a minivan?"

"A minivan?"

"It's not like you couldn't afford it."

"A *minivan*?" Was he missing something here? "To live in?"

"To *carry* things in, Max. Like . . ."

"Like what?"

She glared at him. "Lawn mowers. Gallons of lead-free paint. Tricycles."

He squinted at her, giving it some thought. Either she had a lot of lead-free paint and tricycles she wanted moved around, or the conversation had taken one of those turns where you had to really grip the wheel if you wanted to stay on the road.

This wasn't about tricycles and lead-free paint, he decided, distracted by the way her foot was wiggling. Her skirt had crept up again, not much, but if she kept moving her foot, it might go a little higher. And if he could keep her mind off yanking it down, maybe she'd even uncross her legs, lean toward him, look at him with those soft brown eyes . . .

"Gracie?" he said, trying it out. "You know, now that you mention it, I have been kind of thinking a minivan would be handy."

Her foot stopped wiggling, but the compensation was that her eyes opened wide and she gazed at him with absolute, amazed attention. He had her. At least until she asked him what it would be handy *for*.

"For hauling tricycles," he said. "Or . . . whatever. Lawn mowers."

"You don't have a lawn mower, Max. You don't have a lawn."

It was a point. "Well, if we . . . ah . . ."

The wide-eyed astonishment was changing, just around the edges, to suspicion.

"If I . . . ah, hypothetically . . ."

"What? If you moved out of your apartment and got a place in the suburbs? Settled down? Got married again?"

"*Again?*"

"Is that so unthinkable?"

She'd lost him. The conversation had taken another twist, and he'd missed the corner.

"You know *why* that idea is so unthinkable, Max?" she said. Her tone of voice had moved from mere suspicion to accusatory, I-expected-as-much-but-hoped-for-better hurt feelings. "It's because I'm not sure you ever wanted to get married in the first place."

"Huh?"

"I pushed you into it. I forced you to the altar, Max, because I wanted all the trappings of a real wedding, and the respectability of being married. You really weren't ready—"

"You forced me? Since when?"

"I know you didn't want—"

"You're seriously telling me I didn't want you? Because, seriously, Gracie, that's absolutely—"

"As a wife?"

"Huh?" he said again.

"Did you want me as a *wife*, Max? The family deal? A wife and . . . and . . ."

"Well, hell, yes. Any way I could get you."

She blinked, looking stricken, then reached down for her purse and gathered it into her lap.

"Now, wait a minute, Gracie." He took a step toward her, his hand extended. "I didn't mean that it was just about sex."

"What was it about, then?"

He closed his eyes and pinched the bridge of his nose between thumb and forefinger. This was a test question. He realized that much. But how many possible answers could there be?

He opened his eyes and moved his hand away from his face, then went with the truth, for lack of a better alternative. "We got married because we were in love, Gracie. I mean completely, gonzo, in love."

It must have been all right. She didn't get up and stomp out. Her purse even slipped a bit off her lap. "*Were?*" she repeated tremulously.

He caught the purse as it slid off her thigh, set it back in her lap, then moved his hand a few inches to brush his fingers along her forearm. "Try me, Gracie," he said.

"I already have."

He covered her hand with his, leaned down, touched her hair. "Yeah, well, try me again."

"Max . . ." she said, almost a whisper.

He rested a hand on the back of the chair and moved in to fit their mouths together.

It had been too long. Way too long. He clasped her head, tilting it up to press their mouths closer. She clutched his sleeve, and heat rolled up Max's body in a wave of solid sensuality that could have lit brush fires.

This wasn't just a kiss, he realized with rapidly dissipating coherence. This was Grace. Max Hogan didn't kiss Grace Bennet Hogan as a casual gesture. Two seconds' contact and it was out of control.

There had been plenty of times when they'd made

slow, sensual, postponing-the-pleasure love, or easy, teasing, we've-got-all-afternoon love, but what came to Max's mind at that moment were the times they'd only gotten halfway up the stairs or part way across the living room. Or as far as the office desk.

He traced the curve of her throat, lightly enough to feel the tremor when she sighed and lifted her chin. She went utterly still as his fingers drifted down over her collarbone and slipped into the open neck of her blouse.

"Mmm," she said under his mouth as he undid the first button he came to.

Her grip tightened convulsively on his arm when his fingers drifted into the soft, warm cleft between her breasts, but not, Max thought, with any intention of stopping him. Not with her mouth opening sweetly to let him slip inside and taste her.

He undid another button and made a sound in the back of his throat he hadn't made for months.

Grace heard the strangled moan, and it undid her faster than Max was undoing the buttons on her shirt. She recognized that sound. It had associations that came vibrantly to mind: the two of them entwined on the lace coverlet of their four-poster; Max grinning at her from the backseat of his convertible at the dark end of the long road where he'd taken her parking; Max in the shower with her, soapy hands clasping her backside, her leg hooked over his arm.

She took a deep breath, trying to clear her thoughts, and clutched more tightly to his sleeves. The soft, supple leather yielded under her fingers, stirring more memories with the leather-jacket smell and the hard contours of Max's upper arms. He was murmuring her name in a voice that sounded as if he, too, were viewing the pictures scrolling by her mind's eye.

"Max, we can't do this," she got out.

"What?" he asked hoarsely, his mouth moving against the edge of her jaw. "This?"

"Yes. That."

"We never did this in the . . . office, did we?"

"No. And we can't—"

"That was an oversight, Gracie. But I think"—he undid another button—"we can make that up." The chair tilted slowly as he pressed against it. Grace's feet left the floor. She reacted by holding on to Max as he swiveled the chair so that he could rest the back of it against his desk. With one smooth, slick movement he was suddenly closer to her, down on one knee, his elbow brushing her side as he made the embrace more intimate.

"Max," she said, turning her face away from him. "What are you doing on your knees?"

He paused long enough to peer at her and touch her face with his fingertips, then grinned and murmured, "Proposing?"

Grace felt a shiver travel all the way down her spine as she considered the implications of what he was proposing. He *had* proposed to her on one knee, with a bottle of champagne tucked under his arm and a ring in his jacket pocket. Most of the champagne had gone flat while they marked the occasion in a way that was elementally more satisfying, on a fleece rug in Max's bachelor-furnished apartment.

One high-heeled shoe slipped off as she wiggled her ankle.

Max's palm slipped lightly along the outside of her thigh to the hem of her skirt, slowed down but kept going, brushing her skin through fine nylon, sliding around to the back of her knee to caress her with a bare touch of his fingertips. Her stomach fluttered. It couldn't be fair, could it, that a man she wasn't even living with anymore could know all her most sensitive erogenous zones?

She was almost certain her lawyer wouldn't approve of this.

Grace made a feeble effort to get out from under Max and push herself upright in the chair, but she was fighting against something far stronger than Max's light, knowing hold on her. She could send all the "fight or flight" messages she could think of to her nerve endings; they weren't interested. Every sensory receptor in her body knew exactly what it wanted next.

Max breathed onto the tiny lace flower at the center of her bra, fanning the exquisitely sensitive skin with warm puffs of breath, promising the even warmer, more stirring touch of his mouth. Grace's other shoe fell.

She'd been fooling herself to think she was over him, she realized, somewhere beneath the haze of sensuality that had her mesmerized. Max wasn't the kind of man she could get over in two or three months. Or decades. He was so . . . Max. She could smell the tang of leather from his jacket, feel the soft texture of his hair under her fingers, hear the brush of his knee against the carpet, the rustle of her silk blouse being nuzzled aside . . . the ringing of Max's phone.

Her chair wobbled as Max reached up to the desk, felt around for the phone, and bleeped a little button. He dropped the phone on the desk, but he hadn't gotten to it soon enough to preempt the answering machine, which clicked, whirred, and paused for Max's "not here" message.

A moment later Lillian's voice, altered by the tape machine but still recognizable, said, "Max? Are you there? Pick up, for heaven's sake!"

Max's hand slipped inside her shirt and unfastened the front clasp of her bra. Cool silk shimmered across her breast as he brushed the lacy garment aside. Grace gave an illicit, sensual gasp which sounded even more illicit contrasted with Lillian's voice demanding, "Well, if you're not there, I *hope* I've gotten to you before Grace has."

Clearly, Grace realized, she'd already gotten to him. Or he'd gotten to her. Or something. His warm palm curved around the fullness of her breast, and his breath caressed the sensitive crest. He mumbled something that sounded like her name, in a rough tone of raw emotion, and she felt a shock of dizzying response, turning her body to liquid honey. She was already over the edge, and she knew it.

"She wants to fire you, Max," Lillian's voice squawked. "And I know ordinarily you wouldn't pay any attention to that. At least I *hope* you wouldn't, being the man I think you are, but for *this* time, I want you to go along with it."

Grace frowned and turned her head to stare at the machine, confused. Was that what she was doing? Firing Max? Her hands were inside his jacket roaming over his body, and she'd dipped her fingertips into the back waistband of his pants and inside the elastic band of his underwear. She wanted, badly, to dip a little farther, but somehow it didn't seem right to be jumping Max in his office while listening to her aunt Lillian telling Max she was firing him.

"I was . . . m-m-mistaken about the bottle," Lillian went on. "You don't need to do any more investigating. Especially over the next few days. We wouldn't want to . . . make the family think there was anything amiss."

"Max?" Grace said, pulling her fingers out of his pants. "Isn't that . . . Lillian?"

"Forget Lillian, Gracie. You don't approve of Lillian anyway."

It was true. She didn't. But that wasn't exactly the point, and her wandering common sense was beginning to realize it. The honeyed mist of passion that had wrapped her in erotic oblivion was dissipating, chased by the image of Aunt Lillian—dark hair, brown eyes, expensively manicured nails drumming against the receiver of the phone while she told Max she'd been mistaken in hiring him.

Lillian? Admitting she was mistaken?

"Oh, and Max," Lillian's voice went on, "don't worry about that lightweight, Tedsy. Grace would never fall for someone with so little *machismo*. Just keep her . . . distracted, until, say, the middle of the week. Wednesday, anyway."

Grace felt a blush creeping up to her face from the neckline of her unbuttoned shirt. Max had her distracted, all right. And the way they were going, it would be the middle of next week before either of them realized what week it was.

Max had stopped what he was doing to stare at her with an expression of confusion that mirrored her own. *"Tedsy?"* he said.

She gazed up at Max's sexy, sensually dilated blue eyes and felt a wash of doubt.

She'd come here to fire him. So what was she doing making love to him, in his office, in a swivel chair, on a Saturday afternoon?

"Max," she said huskily, struggling to sit upright, reaching for the floor with her toes and groping for the edges of her blouse with her fingers. "Why does Lillian want me *distracted* until the middle of next week?"

"Distracted?" he repeated. His gaze traveled down the front of her blouse to where her hands clutched it closed. Her husband's baby-blue eyes smoldered with primitive impulses; his features were starkly defined, undeniably marked with purposeful machismo and disbelief at the message she was sending with her body language. The verbal question apparently hadn't penetrated yet.

For a moment the temptation to ignore Lillian's phone message and submit to those persuasive, experienced hands almost overcame her, but the click of the answering machine dragged her back to her senses.

She squirmed up in the tilted chair and caught hold of the desk.

"Who's Tedsy?" Max asked, then before she could answer, held up one hand and made a pained face. "No. Don't tell me. Let me guess. Edmund, right? The estate executor. The bottle salesman." Disgust dripped from his voice. "My wife's consorting with a used bottle salesman called *Tedsy*."

"I'm not *consorting*."

"You're not?"

"No." She wasn't. At least not with Tedsy. She was consorting with her ex-husband, in his office, while her aunt made comments on the answering machine in the background. Sweet chariot! "What are we doing here, Max?" she asked, confused again. "We shouldn't be . . ."

"Oh, now, Gracie, wait a minute."

She squirmed away from him and rolled the chair back by pushing with her toes. Max made a grab for the edge of the desk as she rolled out from under him. "I don't think I have a minute, Max."

"Sure you do. Let's just go back a couple of steps, huh? Maybe back to the—"

"No. No back steps. I mean, maybe I've . . . projected the wrong message here, but—" She fumbled for the edges of her bra, pulled it closed, lost one side, and fumbled again. "But . . ."

Max raised his free hand and inched, on his knees, closer to the desk, where he could prop himself up on one elbow. "Oh, damn. I knew this would happen." He stared at her. "No, I didn't. Why didn't I know this would happen? What am I, dense?"

". . . Max?"

He groaned. "I'm addicted. That's it. I need a twelve-step program."

Her hands slowed on her buttons, and her breath sighed out in a small, guilty whimper.

He groaned again. "Gracie," he murmured, pained. "When you do that, do you have to sound . . . guilty?"

"No. I mean, I'm sorry. I . . ." She stopped, sighed again, and started over. "We shouldn't have done this, Max. Not that it's entirely your fault. I might have been giving you some kind of mixed message, for a moment."

He turned his head slowly to look at her. "That was a *mixed* message?"

She met his gaze, bit her lip, then buttoned another two buttons and tucked in her shirt. "It doesn't change anything, Max. It's just . . ." Her voice trailed off into another guilty whimper.

Max covered his eyes with his hand and let his head drop forward.

She *had* kicked him out, she admitted, and she'd done it at least partly on false pretenses. She'd known all along that Max didn't want anyone but her in his hot tub, just as she couldn't imagine anyone but Max in hers.

Of course, there was the baby in her imminent future. Hot-tubbing as a family activity? She felt a familiar spurt of panic, replacing some of the other emotions churning inside her. The truth was, she hadn't been any more ready than Max was for this unexpected pregnancy. Maybe she still wasn't.

"Max, look," she said, blurting out anything to distract herself from that small-but-threatening-to-get-bigger sense of panic. "Max, I think we're being manipulated—by my aunt."

He didn't move except to draw in a deep breath and release it audibly. "Yeah."

"I think you were right, Max, that Lillian's got some ulterior motive. She's up to something."

"No kidding."

"I know she said I wanted to fire you, and . . . I did, actually, but . . . why does Aunt Lillian want to fire you?"

"Got me," he muttered.

"Maybe you could just do a little investigating, find out what she's up to. My aunt, I mean."

"Call one of her ex-husbands," Max said into his hand.

"I don't want an ex-husband, Max. I want you."

For a long moment he didn't move a muscle. When he lowered his hand to look at her, Grace felt her throat go dry as the meaning of what she'd said burrowed into the core of some emotion that threatened to gush up into the very air. She hadn't meant it, of course. It was just a slip of the tongue, a missed meaning. She'd meant she needed him as a detective. A business arrangement.

"I'll pay you," she said.

His head jerked back as if she'd kicked him in the

forehead. "You'll pay me," he said expressionlessly, then, as if she'd just suggested blowing up the White House, "You'll *pay* me?" He jerked his gaze from hers and pounded his clenched fist against his chest, eliciting a small cough. "She'll pay me," he muttered. He pulled open the lower file cabinet drawer and rummaged around in it, coming up with a pint bottle. He shut the drawer, dropped onto his backside on the floor, leaned against the cabinet, then broke the seal on the bottle and upended it.

"Max? What are you doing?"

"It's medicine, Grace." He took another swig, capped the bottle, then set it up on the desk beside his head, his eyes closed.

"Medicine? For what?"

"Ex-spousal contact."

She was up out of the chair and had snagged the bottle before he got a hand anywhere close to rescuing it.

"You're drinking! In the middle of the afternoon!"

"It doesn't happen often, Grace. In fact, it never happened until now."

"Until this contact with your *ex-spouse*?"

"Yeah," he said, as if he wondered what else she expected him to say. "Until I came into contact with my ex-spouse."

"I'm not sure how I feel about that statement, Max Hogan!"

He frowned at her, his gaze moving from the bottle she had clutched against her chest to the indeterminate expression on her face.

"Guilty?" he suggested finally.

She stared at him, shifted her weight back and forth between her two stockinged feet, then raised the bottle to her lips and took a healthy swallow.

Max had always had a knack for putting his finger on the obvious part of the truth.

Ex-spousal contact could drive a woman to drink.

FOUR

Aunt Lillian's housekeeper was a hard sell, Grace thought with chagrin. She hefted her Waterford crystal prop, murmured, "Chocolate mousse," and crunched a loose edge of aluminum foil down around the punch bowl.

Mrs. Willoford frowned at it.

"I'll just pop this in the refrigerator," Grace went on, gesturing up the marble-and-steel-cantilevered stairs of her aunt's foyer, "and leave Aunt Lillian a note. Oh, and I promised her I'd get out the Danish crystal. You don't have to wait for me. I'll let myself out and lock up."

"Danish crystal?" Mrs. Willoford said repressively.

"She's entertaining tonight. He's a chocolate lover."

"Another one?"

"Another one."

Mrs. Willoford huffed like an impending Florida

squall, but she stepped back onto the porch when Grace made a move to close the front door. Through the narrow venetian blinds she watched the woman march down the drive, disapproval evident in the line of her back, returning to the caretaker's cottage she rented from Lillian.

Grace let out her breath, turned, and climbed half a flight of black marble stairs to her aunt's living room. It had been redone the year before in burgundy, black, and chrome, with modern Japanese prints. All the furniture had steel legs, a fact which made Grace uneasy in an indefinable way. She'd gotten used to wood, old glass, and fabric faded in a slow, dignified way. She was an antiques dealer. A businesswoman with a respectable reputation. Good heavens, what was she doing here, sneaking around in her aunt's house?

Max should be the one doing this.

The thought slithered in under her defenses like a flu virus, and she caught herself just about to inhale it.

No, her ex-husband should not be involved in this investigation of Lillian. That was one thing he'd been right about. Two things, if she included his suspicions about the case. Three, if she admitted she was feeling guilty.

Grace shut her eyes again and clutched the aluminum-foil-wrapped crystal to her bosom, unsure whether it was her conscience or the edge of the punch bowl that was jabbing her in the ribs.

Sweet chariot. Subterfuge was nerve-racking.

For two months she had justified her keeping a secret from Max with indignation and, truth to tell, self-righteous superiority. But it was hard to feel self-righteous when three days earlier she'd had her hand in her husband's pants; and now, standing in her aunt's living room gripping her punch bowl, she had to admit that maybe, maybe, she was being a little hard on Max.

True, he hadn't so far shown any great potential for parenthood, but who was she to talk? How was she to know she had any better knack for it than Aunt Lillian, who, at least, had the advantage of indestructible self-esteem and undiluted enthusiasm for being a parent?

Not that she herself didn't, Grace clarified in her mind. She *did* want this child. Very much. She wanted to have it, nurture it, give it the best possible start, be the best possible mother . . .

That niggling thread of panic that never quite went away vibrated anew in the pit of her stomach, mixed up now with the guilt she felt about kicking Max out, letting him back in, consorting with him in a swivel chair with the kind of passionate abandon that could have cast Lillian in the shade.

She squeezed her eyes shut tighter, then opened them and stared down at the aluminum foil sliding off the edge of her punch bowl. "Oh, Lord," she said aloud, feeling a little relief in the spoken words. "Feeling guilty is so *exhausting*!"

"Either that, or carrying around a ten-pound punch bowl," Max said.

Her eyes flew open, her mouth dropped, and the bowl wobbled in her hands. "Max?"

He skipped toward her along the gallery-hallway, making a dive for the punch bowl.

"I've got it," she snapped, wrapping her arms around the crystal bowl. "I'm capable of carrying a bowl of mousse, for Pete's sake." She'd better be, that persistent, anxiety-inducing voice in her head pointed out. In a few short months she'd have a baby to carry.

"Just trying to help."

"What are you doing here, anyway?"

"Spying on Lillian." He reached out to straighten the aluminum foil, which had gone askew, then pushed his hands into his pockets when she glared at him. "What are *you* doing here?" he asked.

There didn't seem to be much point in answering, since she was caught red-handed and had already admitted she was guilty of something.

"I thought you asked *me* to spy on Lillian," he said.

"I thought you said *no*."

He scowled at her, his eyes darkening with something she would have sworn, a moment ago, she had a monopoly on: indignation. "Well, I did, but—" He shrugged, looking pained by the attempt at explanation, then he lowered his gaze to the bowl. "What is this stuff, anyway?" he asked, reaching out to lift the foil.

"Mousse."

"Moose?"

"It's *Mousse au Chocolat*, Max."

He flicked the foil off, then, staring down at the bowl, stuck his finger into the center of it, rooting around. "Jeez, Gracie." His tone was one of offended incredulity. "What'd you do with the fish?"

"I did not put Lucifer in the *pudding*, Max!" She

yanked the bowl away from him. "What do you take me for?"

He didn't argue the point, apparently satisfied there were no bodies in the punch bowl. He stuck his finger into his mouth. "Hey. This is pretty good. What'd you say it was?"

"Actually, it's instant chocolate pudding. I needed chocolate."

"Chocolate?"

"To fool Mrs. Willoford."

He raised an eyebrow.

"Lillian thinks chocolate is sexy," she explained.

The other eyebrow rose. Max's gaze slipped away from hers, wandered across the carpet, wandered back, stopped at her Reeboks, then made a leisurely, elaborately casual pass up the length of her body until he met her eyes again. "Sexy," he said, with no particular intonation.

But with his eyes darkening to that sexy, sensual shade of blue Grace knew only too well, he didn't need any intonation.

Or maybe it was her, she decided, feeling a wave of heat drift up from the soles of her feet to wash a delicate blush across her cheekbones. Sweet chariot, they were incorrigible, weren't they? A passing mention of chocolate, and they were both thinking of swivel chairs and Lucifer's ecstasy.

But at least she wasn't feeling guilty anymore, she realized. She was feeling . . . stirred up. Alive. Aware. Admit it or not, Max stirred sparks that made her conscience sit down and shut up. She'd spent two months acting responsible and domestic, but one visit from Max and she was subterfuging her way into Lillian's house and planning on snooping through her files.

Lillian would have been proud of her.

"All right, Max," she said, brushing by him and marching down the hall toward Lillian's study. "What have you found out?"

He followed her, but when she reached the study, she realized he'd stopped several paces back. He was standing at the doorway to her old bedroom, peering into it with a thoughtful frown, as if it might hold clues to his investigation.

Curious, she walked back to him and gazed into the room. It had been recently redecorated, in purple and khaki with iridescent gold accents.

Max glanced at her. "Wasn't this room green the last time I looked at it?"

"Aunt Lillian was struck by inspiration a couple of months ago."

"An inspiration for what? To run off and join the circus?" He leaned into the room to get a better look. "She got a fortune-teller or something stashed in the closet?"

Grace chuckled self-consciously. "She told me she wanted to 'maintain its whimsical character as a child's room.' In case—" She hesitated, then finished the sentence on one breath. "In case there were any more children in her life."

"Where's she think she's going to get 'em? Snag one from a couple of gypsies passing through town?"

Grace's heart stopped beating, momentarily arrested by the mixed onslaught of guilt, panic, and hurt at Max's oblivious assumption that the future children in Lillian's life would not be theirs.

He glanced toward her, then straightened, his expression alarmed and regretful. "Oh, dammit, Grace, I'm sorry. I didn't mean . . . you."

"Me?" The word had almost no voice behind it.

"I mean, your parents leaving you with Lillian. I didn't mean your parents."

"My *parents*?"

"Yeah." He appeared confused. "Wasn't that what . . . why you looked so . . . ?"

She closed her eyes, feeling another rush of conflicting emotion: appreciation that Max understood and cared about her feelings toward her own parents, exasperation that he *didn't* understand what was going on now, and relief that she wasn't, after all, going to have to tell him. Yet.

"Grace?"

She shook her head. "No. It's all right, Max. About my parents."

"But . . ."

"What have you found out about Lillian?"

He shifted his weight from one foot to the other, studying her, then apparently decided to let her change the subject. "Not too much. Whatever she's into, she's not keeping records. The phone company is, though." He reached into his back pocket and pulled out a folded stack of papers. "And on her last phone bill, there are a few interesting calls."

"Like what?" Grace asked. She thrust the bowl of pudding toward him and reached for the bill.

"That four-oh-four-nine number?" he said. "That's Eloise Goodbody."

"Eloise Goodbody? Aunt Lillian's ex-sister-in-law?"

"That's right. One-half heiress to the Goodbody estate. And until all this came down, I wasn't aware that Eloise and Lillian were especially close friends."

Grace shrugged doubtfully. "I think they were friendly when Lillian was married to Martin and Eloise was married to Martin's older brother. But . . ."

"Yeah, well, Lillian's reached out to Eloise a dozen times in the past three weeks, since Martin died. And I don't think all of it has to do with shared sympathy and support."

"No," Grace admitted. "As an ex-husband, Martin was way down on Lillian's list. I think they had some kind of disagreement in the divorce that was never resolved."

"So how come Lillian's talking to Eloise three times a week?"

"They must be talking about the estate. But what is there to talk about? It all goes to auction, with the proceeds divided equally between Marian and Eloise. Cut-and-dried."

Max juggled the punch bowl in one hand and took the phone bill back. "Not counting Tedsy's cut, of course. Remember Tedsy?"

"Of course I remember him. His name is Edmund."

"Yeah. Edmund. Has he made any interesting overtures lately?"

"Overtures? To me? I don't know what you're talking about."

Max glanced down at the bowl of chocolate pudding again, assessed her delicately flushed face, then reached behind him and set the bowl on the third step. He slid his hands into his pockets, facing her, and rocked back on his heels. "If you really don't know what I'm talking about, Gracie," he said softly, "I could show you the moves."

Her throat dried, and her hands dampened. They'd been talking about Lillian's phone bill, hadn't they? How had they gotten onto this particular topic?

"This . . . uh, isn't a good idea, Max," she muttered.

"What isn't?"

"This . . . kind of talk."

He was silent long enough for a couple of racy, flush-enhancing images to cross her mind.

"Yeah," he agreed finally. Before she had a chance to feel a sense of relief, though, he added, "But what's that got to do with it?"

"What's—"

"Gracie, two people don't get it on because it's a *good idea*."

Her mouth wrinkled as she tried to think of an answer.

Max's mouth wrinkled too. "With the possible exception of Tedsy," he added.

"For Pete's sake, Max," she burst out, exasperated. "Would you forget about Tedsy?"

"I'd like to forget about Tedsy. I'd like it even better if you forgot about him. Matter of fact, what I'd really like is if we both forgot about him."

"Well, then—"

"How about it, Gracie?" he asked, his voice dropping to a rough, persuasive murmur. "We forget about everyone else except you and me. Just the two of us, alone. Because what happens when we're alone together, Gracie, is—"

"Stop it, Max. Just stop right there," she said, holding up one hand like a traffic cop.

"Why? You can't deny it. Every time we're together—"

"I know! All right. Okay. I know what happens when we're alone together. You don't have to—"

"Not just when we're together, Gracie. We don't even have to be together for me to be thinking about you, about what we do to each other. Hell, I don't even have to be awake. Do you know what that's like, Gracie?"

His eyes had gone dark, the way they did when he was aroused, but it wasn't sexual passion that Grace read on his face. Not entirely. He wanted an answer to his question, she realized, surprised. He wanted to know if she shared his obsession.

There was no safe way to answer him. Her emotions were pooling somewhere in the center of her chest, where her heart was beating in slow, hard thuds.

"Ah, Gracie . . ." He took a step toward her.

Grace steadied herself with a hand on the banister and one foot behind her on the lowest stair.

"You know how many women I've even thought about being with since I met you?"

"You mean aside from the blonde in the hot tub?"

He looked hurt. "Come on, Grace. You know damn well I wasn't fooling around with some bimbo saleslady when I could have been fooling around with you."

She dragged air into her lungs, holding his gaze, mesmerized. "I know that," she admitted.

"Yeah. You've got to know that, Gracie. Because it isn't logic, and it isn't just, you know, the rules."

"What is it, then?" she asked, backing a couple of steps up the staircase, skirting the bowl.

Max took a couple of steps too. "It's . . . internal combustion. It's something that happens when we're in the same room. Or the same town. Same planet. I didn't ask for it, you didn't ask for it, but we got it. Maybe it's not what we would have planned for, but that's the way it is."

Good God, Grace thought. Was he talking about . . . ? Her heart started to pound with heavy jolts of emotion. Was he about to tell her he'd figured things out, that he'd put the clues together and was ready to . . . to . . .

The sound of tires crunching on gravel provided a minor but insistent intrusion on her thoughts.

Max frowned, turning his head slightly toward the sound. "What's that?"

"It sounds like a car," Grace said.

"Lillian?"

The car drew to a halt. A door slammed, and footsteps crunched up the walkway.

"I don't think it's Lillian," Max said.

It wasn't. Lillian wouldn't bang on the front door and call out, "Police. Open up."

Grace reached down to pick up the punch bowl and clutched it to her chest, stilling panic. "It's the police," she hissed at Max.

"No kidding," he mouthed back.

"What are we going to do?"

"I don't know. You got any great ideas?"

"The back way?"

"Grace, babe, they've already seen your car. Not to mention mine."

"*Yours?* You brought your own car to break into Lillian's house?"

"Yeah."

"Well, for God's sake, Max—"

"What? You didn't bring your car?"

"Well, all right, I did, but—"

"All right then. Answer the door, Grace. I'll hold the punch bowl."

She hurried down the hallway to the foyer, telling herself she could handle this, but she had to wipe her palm against her skirt before she reached for the doorknob.

Standing on the other side of the door was an official-looking uniformed policeman, an idling police car, and Mrs. Willoford.

"Is Ms. Bennet home?" the officer asked.

Grace cleared her throat. "No. She's not. I'm her

niece. Grace Bennet . . . ah . . . Hogan. Can I help you?"

"Uh-huh," the man said. "You could tell us what you're doing here."

"I'm . . . stocking the refrigerator," Grace improvised. "I brought over a chocolate mousse."

"You mind if we check that out, Ms. Hogan?" He gestured behind him. "Your aunt's housekeeper thought you were taking an unjustifiably long time to drop off the food." In the driveway, Mrs. Willoford stood beside the cruiser, arms crossed in front of her meager chest, looking suspicious and determined. Either Aunt Lillian had told her not to trust anyone, Grace thought, or over the course of working for Lillian she'd come to that conclusion herself.

"Uh . . . no, of course I don't mind." Sweet chariot! What was she supposed to say? "Now where did I put that . . . ?"

"The mousse?" Max said, from the top of the stairs. "Right here."

"And who," the policeman asked pointedly, "is this?"

Grace glanced from Max to the police officer, rising dread filling her chest and closing her throat.

"Ms. Hogan?" the policeman prompted.

"This is . . . my ex-husband," she said. "Sort of."

The policeman gave her a jaded, deadpan look. Clearly, as a criminal, she wasn't much of a challenge. From the top of the stairs, Max's audible sigh expressed more or less the same sentiment. Mrs. Willoford uncrossed her arms, looking smug.

"I think," the cop said, "you'd both better come with me."

Two hours and quite a lot of questions later, Max opened the police station door for Grace and they walked out into the sunshine, sprung. Lillian had been unavailable for consultation, since she had not, in fact, been playing cards with her bridge group, but Max had reached Ernie, who'd gotten them out.

Grace hadn't said much of anything at all to Max since her "Ex-husband sort of" comment, but that comment had been echoing in his mind for the past two hours. What had she meant by the *sort of* part? Was she taking back the *ex* in the ex-husband designation? Should he ask her?

"Gracie—"

"Max—"

They fell silent simultaneously, Max trying to phrase his question, Grace chewing her lower lip. She spoke again first.

"I guess I should thank you for getting us out of trouble."

"We weren't in that much trouble, anyway. Lillian wouldn't have pressed charges. I don't think."

"I should have suspected Mrs. Willoford might call the authorities."

"You're not the suspecting type, Gracie. You have trusting written all over you. Anyone but Mrs. Willoford would have taken one look at you and assumed innocence."

She smiled ruefully. "I guess I don't really have any aptitude for deception."

"Yeah, well, you're damn good at a lot of other things, babe."

She shot him a quick, startled glance, as if she were about to ask *Like what?* but thought better of it.

"An honest streak isn't that much of a fault, Gracie. In fact—" He stopped halfway down the stone steps and turned toward her, his hands in his pockets. "It's . . ."

". . . What?"

Sexy as hell, he was about to say. Especially when it applied to taking the *ex* out of ex-husband.

"Never mind," she said with a sigh, before he could speak. "Maybe I could work on developing some of Aunt Lillian's better qualities."

"What better qualities?"

"I could become more adventurous, for example."

Adventurous? He stared at her, perplexed, recalling a couple of late-night sofa incidents that could have taught "adventurous" to Arnold Schwarzenegger. "You're adventurous enough, Grace."

"As opposed to domestic enough?"

"You're domestic enough too."

"How do you know that?" The soft brown eyes were wide, their expression troubled and sincere. Max felt his heart skip a little faster just at the sight of them. She even leaned toward him, half reaching for his forearm, passionate in her wish to communicate. He didn't have a clue what exactly she was communicating, however. "How do *I* know that, Max?" she asked, her voice entreating.

"But . . . that's what you do, Gracie. Refinishing furniture, selling antiques, all that stuff."

"That's just . . . redecorating, Max. *Lillian* redecorates."

She sighed again. "When I first moved in with Aunt Lillian the one thing I liked about my room was that it had blue walls, the same as the walls in my bedroom in my family's old house. Even though I was fifteen and in high school I put up all my grammar-school posters of teddy bears and dolls. And I had this little fairy princess night-light that I'd gotten for my tenth birthday. And my old bedspread."

Max's frown softened at the thought of the little girl Grace had been, shunted around from place to place, bringing her treasures with her.

"A month and a half after I moved in with Lillian, I went on a sleep-over with some friends I'd made at school. And when I came back, Aunt Lillian had gone in and redecorated." She smiled ruefully, but Max could tell the smile was a cover-up for a memory that still hurt.

"Everything was done over in rose and silver. New bed, bedspread, bureau, pink walls. Aunt Lillian hadn't spared any expense with it. She was sure I'd be delighted."

"And you weren't," Max ventured.

Grace took a deep breath. "Oh, I was, but . . . I wanted it the old way. Maybe it wasn't age-appropriate or stylish or even very appealing, but it was my attempt to be domestic, I guess."

He reached toward her, then stopped himself, wanting badly to hold her, but not sure she'd let him. "She shouldn't have done that to you, babe," he said. "She should have left all your old stuff there, where you wanted it. She shouldn't have . . . hurt you that way."

"Oh—" She shrugged. "It was just furniture, after all. That's not what's really important in life. It doesn't make you a good person or a good . . ."

A good what? he wondered.

"The women in my family aren't domestic, Max. My mother, Lillian. They don't set up family households and plant vegetable gardens and have babies."

He frowned, taking in her body language, the passionate tone of voice, the emotion in her eyes. Half his mind was still distracted with the late-night sofa images. The other half was making a stab at figuring out what she was saying. This was like the minivan conversation, he realized. But a little more . . . biological. They were talking about babies, not minivans. The women in her family didn't have babies?

"Well, Grace," he said finally, "some of them must have had babies."

"Oh, Max." She let out a big breath, covered her face with her hands, then started down the steps again.

"What?" he said.

She waved at him, turning away as she kept walking. "I'll talk to Lillian as soon as she gets home and tell her what I was doing there. She'll probably just assume you came along with me."

"Wait a minute, Gracie. I mean, just—"

She paused again at the bottom of the steps, looking at him for a moment, her expression vulnerable. Max felt something tighten in his chest, around the region of his heart.

" 'Bye, Max," she said softly, then started toward her car, which the police had driven to the station for her. Max's own car was still stashed a quarter of a mile from Lillian's. He'd figured Grace would offer him a ride to pick it up, but as he watched her walk away from him, the problem of getting his car back was not foremost in his mind. The problem of getting his wife back took precedence, and mulling that over took all his attention.

He knew that Grace wanted a family, eventually. They hadn't gotten around to talking about it, though, and truth to tell, he had felt more relief than anything. What was the hurry, anyway, in having babies?

Max himself was the youngest in a family of six, the tail-end, afterthought kid. He'd been an uncle since he was eight; all five of his siblings had kids already. There didn't seem to be much of a trick to having 'em. It was raising them Max wasn't sure he was up to.

But Grace? He hadn't suspected Grace of having doubts about her abilities as a mother. He'd figured her as a natural. Still did. Grace with a baby. A little girl, maybe, with Grace's eyes. Grace pushing her on a swing, laughing with her, buying her a chocolate bar. He stuck his hands into his pockets and hunched his shoulders, aware of an odd, tight feeling in his chest.

Did you feed babies chocolate? Probably not, he

figured. Until they had teeth, anyway. Although they could probably gum down chocolate mousse. But was that the sort of thing you fed babies? Did it give them future cavities?

He had plenty of his own doubts, he had to admit. And he could see, he supposed, how a woman whose domestic models had been her globe-trotting parents and her aunt Lillian might have doubts herself.

But how badly could Lillian have done? She'd raised Grace, hadn't she?

And look how Grace had turned out.

FIVE

"This is it, Eloise. I'm not making another trip up Marian's damn attic stairs."

"What'd you expect? An escalator?"

"*Marian* certainly doesn't climb these narrow stairs. I doubt that she'd fit between the railings."

"She must make Edmund do it."

"And after we get it all over to Martin's house, we're going to have to carry it all up to *his* attic. That's at least as many trips as we've already made getting it out to this truck. And I've chipped one nail as it is."

"So you have," Eloise said. There was a suspiciously sardonic note in her voice. "That'll be a hard circumstance to explain, given your lifestyle."

Lillian slanted a sour glance at her.

"All right," Eloise said as they slammed the tailgate shut. "Let's go. I've wiped the place for prints and locked up behind us. Marian won't be any the wiser when she gets back from Mah Jong, and Martin's attic shouldn't give us any trouble, aside from a few cob-webs."

"I'm sure you should know," Lillian said, starting the truck. "Since you've been up in that attic before."

Eloise made a noncommittal grunt and squirmed around to examine the item lying on the backseat. "So this is it," she said, pulling off the quilted covering Lillian had carefully wrapped around the painting she'd just looted from Marian's attic.

"Be careful with it."

"Just looking."

"Didn't you look at it when Marian bribed you to steal it from Martin?"

"That was so long ago I've forgotten what it looks like."

"It wasn't *that* long ago."

Eloise snorted. "Martin was what? Your third hus-band? That would make you about . . . mid-forties when he had this painted?"

"I haven't kept track of exact dates," Lillian said vaguely.

"All I can say is, you've covered quite a time span for a woman who claims to be fifty-two."

"Fifty-one."

"Well, let me see. You divorced Martin in—"

"The point is, Eloise, he should have *given* me the painting in the divorce settlement. It's a portrait of *me*, after all."

"Wanted to keep it, I imagine. The horny old buz-zard."

"He *was* very attached to it," Lillian said, smiling fondly.

"Not to mention that he enjoyed sticking it in Marian's craw. Marian *is* a tad too *respectable*."

"Well," Lillian said sweetly, "she has to be respectable for all of you, doesn't she?"

"Respectable, my foot. She's the one who wanted the painting swiped from Martin. Couldn't stand the thought of her black sheep brother drooling over a painting of his black sheep ex-wife, no offense, Lillian. And *then* she stiffed me on the Tiffany lamps she promised me as payment."

Lillian shot a glance over her shoulder at the back of the vehicle. "Are you sure she promised you this many?"

"Well, if they're going into the estate with everything else, I had to take twice as many, since I only get half the proceeds."

Lillian frowned at her, momentarily derailed by the logic.

"So, Lillian, your painting will go back into the estate too. You planning to buy it when it comes up at auction?"

"Mm."

"What's that mean—mm?"

"Actually, if you must know, I'm hoping to buy it privately, before the estate gets auctioned off. If Grace is in charge of the appraising, she can set a value on it, and we can arrange something."

"The will stipulates that everything goes into the estate sale, Lillian," Eloise told her skeptically. "And

Grace, well, she's a lovely girl, and I'm sure she's your favorite niece, but she's awfully *honest*, isn't she?"

"I know. But really, she's got to see reason in this. What if the price goes sky-high? Who knows what some . . . collector will be willing to bid?"

"On *this*?" Eloise jerked the covering off. "Good God, Lillian. The artist's made you look like an overblown Gina Lollobrigida. With implants."

Lillian scowled, peeked at the painting, then raised her eyebrows and straightened her shoulders. "I think it's a rather good likeness," she said.

Was Edmund Goodbody making a pass at her?

Grace tried to gauge the expectant smile with which he'd just proposed getting her a cup of coffee. The offer wouldn't have merited a second thought, except that Edmund's prep-school grin had taken on a shy, hopeful glint she hadn't noticed before.

"No, thank you."

He looked disappointed. "Some other time, then."

Grace studied him, still uncertain of his intentions. Was she imagining things? Was Max getting to her, with his Tedsy theories?

She gave the idea of marrying Edmund a brief run through her imagination. He was, she supposed, an attractive man—in an aging-Hugh Grant, Ivy-League-polish sort of way. A little too polite maybe, or too civilized, or . . . responsible. Or something.

The fact was, she was already married.

Sort of. But Max was the kind of man who seemed to stick in one's psyche.

"I have to tell you, Grace," Edmund said, "that I'm very pleased with the interest you've generated in my flask."

"Yes, I'm happy with the turnout," Grace agreed.

Both of them glanced toward the small knot of pre-auction viewers clustered around Edmund's bitters flask. Grace had arranged for it to be sold in the Associated Auctioneers' annual Gala Glassware sale, which drew buyers from all over New England.

The crowd was lively, she noted, but her complacency was almost immediately ruffled as she got a better look. Antiques collectors were on the whole an eccentric lot and dressed accordingly, but . . . black leather jacket? White T-shirt? Ray•Bans?

The subject in question raised his head and lifted his sunglasses, fixed her with a smoldering blue gaze, and stopped her breathing for at least fifteen seconds.

He probably knew it too. A smile was creeping up the corners of his mouth. He pushed his hands into the pockets of his jeans, shrugged innocently, and smirked at her, the very picture of an estranged husband casually perusing a glassware auction, where the presence of his glassware-dealing wife was entirely coincidental.

Grace took a deep breath—replenishing her oxygen supply—and turned back to Edmund. "Well," she said, making an effort at conversation, "I expect the bidding on your flask to exceed the estimate by at least twenty percent."

He smiled, left his tie in perfect twelve o'clock position, and flicked a charmingly interested glance over her figure, although in strict courtesy he didn't venture below the second button of her blouse.

The same couldn't be said of Max, who, she noticed, was bearing down upon them, glowering with all the subtlety of a neon sign in an antique shop window.

"Grace," he said, stepping up to her side.

She turned her head and made an uncharacteristic fluttering Victorian gesture with her hand. "Max."

Edmund, glancing from one to the other, put in the first word. "How do you do?" he said politely.

Max nodded at him.

"Edmund, this is . . . M-M-Max," Grace stammered.

Edmund waited politely for her to complete the introduction.

"My . . . er . . ."

"Potential cell mate?" Max murmured.

"Ah," Edmund said. "You're a seller?"

"Not exactly," Max replied.

"Oh. I thought you said—"

"Let me put it this way, Edmund. I'm definitely not letting go of anything that's mine."

"Ah," Edmund said. "A buyer. Well. You're in good company."

"That's debatable," Max muttered.

"Not at all. Grace"—Edmund beamed at her—"has done an exemplary job of moving this bottle. I'm sure, if you're a seller, her services would meet with your approval."

"Oh, Grace has moved my bottles, all right. Quite a few times."

"Max," Grace said, finding her voice, "if you're here hoping to have your bottles moved, you're in the wrong place at the wrong time."

Her ex-husband turned his cobalt-blue gaze on her, made it go dramatically dark, and asked, "Should I make an appointment?"

"No," she said, her voice higher than normal. She cleared her throat. "I don't have my appointment schedule with me."

"Don't give me that line, Gracie. You're woman enough to make an appointment when you want to, no matter what your *schedule* is."

"If I *had* made an appointment, it wouldn't be here, and it wouldn't be now!"

To her surprise, he stared at her in silence instead of making an immediate retort. Then he pushed his hands into his pockets and asked, "When would it be?"

She didn't answer, and he tipped his head to one side, peering at her with a speculative expression. "Suppose I made a killing on bottles and bought a minivan, Gracie. When would it be you'd want to move all those tricycles?"

Her heart stopped beating for a moment—she could have sworn it did—and all the breath in her lungs suddenly stuck there as her throat closed. "I didn't think you were interested in tricycles, Max."

He frowned, perplexed and still unenlightened, she realized. Relief and disappointment sharpened her reactions.

"What are you *doing* here, Max?"

He shrugged. "I'm looking for Lillian."

"Lillian?"

"Lillian?" Edmund put in.

"Lillian," Max said again.

"I saw her at the snack bar a few minutes ago," Edmund said helpfully. "I thought it was Grace. They have the same coloring and delicate features. It's quite striking."

"I think I could manage to tell them apart," Max commented.

"Well. Be that as it may, I believe she's still at the snack bar."

Max gave Edmund a black glare, slid a smoldering visual promise over Grace, and backed off. Grace watched him retreat, half a head taller than most of the other men in the room, his stride half a foot longer, his attitude half feral and half possessive alpha male. One step away from . . . paternalistic.

She wrapped her hands around her middle, taking deep, Lamaze-type breaths.

"So, Max, is it?" Edmund said. "He's Lillian's . . . latest?"

Grace turned back to Edmund, blowing out a breath and resisting the urge to pant.

"Ah . . . forgive me for bringing her up," Edmund added.

"What should I forgive you for?"

"Well—" He smiled and gave a short, understanding chuckle. "I've had that type in my family too."

What was he talking about? He'd had Lillian herself in his family, never mind her "type."

"Certain women," Edmund continued, "will always go for that kind of . . . animal appeal, you know."

"Are you talking about Lillian?"

"Oh, yes. But I wouldn't worry too much. Lillian is up to it, if anyone is."

Grace gave him a blank stare. Lillian? And Max?

"It takes a woman like Lillian to handle a man like Max," Edmund pronounced complacently.

Grace shot another distracted gaze toward the man in question, opened her eyes wide, and suddenly realized the direction of Edmund's insinuations.

"Oh, no, it doesn't," she snapped.

Max caught up with Lillian at the coffee bar where she was drinking café latte and scribbling figures in her auction catalog beside Lot 46, the bitters flask. Her dark hair, a little more auburn than usual, was swept back into a perfect shoulder-skimming coif. She wore the kind of knit dress that had no shape of its own, which wasn't a problem for Lillian. She had plenty of shape for anything she wore.

The sum in her auction catalog looked like twenty-six thousand dollars, Max noted, peering at it over her shoulder.

She flashed him a bland smile and casually dropped the catalog on the coffee bar, where, no doubt, other potential bidders could fortuitously catch sight of the figure and upwardly revise their own estimates.

"Does Grace know you're helping her out this way with your margin notes, Lillian?" he asked her.

"Oh, I don't bother Grace with every little detail." Lillian gave a breezy flip of her fingers, then subjected her nails to a brief critical examination before she picked up her latte. "She has so much on her mind lately."

"Yeah? What?"

Lillian didn't answer, and Max's brooding gaze wandered toward the blush-pink dress across the room.

Grace was still talking to Tedsy the boyish charmer, but at least she was no longer batting her eyelashes and flapping her hands like a geisha girl. She glanced once toward the bitters flask, then turned back toward Edmund. Her short pink dress clung to her backside as she shifted her weight in her high heels. Unlike Lillian's attire, the pink dress wasn't particularly suggestive, but hell, how much suggestion did a man need?

He looked back at Lillian. "Has Grace been involved in some kind of business deal that meant she had to move a lot of . . . tricycles, Lillian?"

Grace's aunt turned her head toward him and raised first one eyebrow, then the other.

"Forget it," Max said.

A futile directive. Lillian inspected him from beneath her raised eyebrows. "Is that what you've been doing with Grace?" she asked, sounding mildly disappointed. "Talking about business deals?"

"Not exactly."

"Well, what *have* you been talking about?"

Max's gaze moved from the raised eyebrows to the

raised chin, to the little cup she was holding and the tips of her red-painted fingernails. She'd broken one of her nails doing some damn thing he couldn't imagine. The heaviest manual labor Lillian engaged in was picking up a hand of poker, and he happened to know she hadn't been at her card game last Tuesday, where he also happened to know bridge wasn't the game of choice.

Max leaned both elbows on the coffee bar behind him. "Lillian," he asked, "the first time you redecorated Grace's room, did you throw out all the stuff she brought with her?"

"Her things? You mean when she moved in when she was fifteen?"

"Yeah. A little fairy princess night-light, for instance?"

Lillian frowned at him. "Are you trying to tell me, Maxwell, that you and Grace broke in to my house, rummaged around when I wasn't there, to find a *night-light*?"

"Where were you, by the way?"

"I play bridge on Tuesdays."

"You weren't at the card game, Lillian. And it's not bridge. It's poker."

Lillian sipped from her latte cup and gave Max the benefit of an indignantly raised eyebrow. "Actually, I had lunch with a friend, last Tuesday."

"A friend? Eloise Goodbody, maybe?"

The latte cup clattered against the saucer, but Lillian managed a credibly casual return of his stare. "What makes you think I've been in touch with my ex-sister-in-law?"

"I read your phone bill."

"My *phone bill*?" She stiffened on her stool, straightening herself to her full height, which wasn't impressive, and showing to best advantage her figure, which was. "Grace didn't tell me you took my phone bill!"

"I didn't take it. I just looked at it."

"That's invasion of privacy!"

Max grinned at her. This from a woman who invaded privacy three times a day just to keep in practice. "Don't worry, Lillian. We'll keep all this in the family."

Lillian opened her mouth, thought better of her intended comment, and said, "Mm."

"It's tacky," he continued, "involving the law in your personal in-law squabbles."

"Mm," Lillian said.

"And particularly when there's an inheritance under question, from, say, an ex-husband."

"Mm," Lillian said again, with restraint.

Max sighed. "I was hoping for more of a comment, tell you the truth."

"Well, Max, if I knew exactly what you were getting at, I might have more to say about it."

"If I knew exactly what I was getting at, Lillian, I wouldn't have to grill you."

"No." She picked up her latte, her hands once again steady, her smile complacent. "I guess you wouldn't, would you?"

Max grunted. Lillian had the undented self-confidence of a born criminal. They were all lucky she hadn't turned her hand to anything truly nefarious. "I hear you called Ernie the other day."

"Oh, that was purely social. An interesting man, your friend Ernie."

"I know."

"He loves chocolate."

"He does?"

Lillian smiled, a cat-with-the-cream expression that gave Max pause. Ernie had passed the chocolate test? *Lillian's* chocolate test?

Maybe Max should warn him. He frowned. Should he? Ernie wasn't dense. He generally knew what was going on.

Still, any man whose idea of reconciliation was to let your ex-wife bean you with a crystal punch bowl—should he be left on his own with the likes of Lillian?

On the other hand, Ernie had been right about the guilt thing.

Maybe.

Max's gaze wandered again toward Grace, who was still, he noted darkly, talking to Edmund. About business, Max reminded himself. Grace wasn't interested in Edmund. She was interested in Max.

He knew that for a fact. There was that sexy, husky catch in her voice whenever the conversation got personal. And the way her brown eyes got soft and luminous, and her breathing quickened.

He knew for a fact she wasn't thinking about beaning him with a punch bowl. It was only a matter of time before things . . . developed. Before she dropped that *ex* part in the ex-husband, and the possibilities of that pink dress could be appreciated in the kind of leisurely, sensual . . .

"Got your eye on anything, Max?"

"Huh?"

"In the auction. Any glassware?" Lillian's brown eyes widened with what would have passed for innocence in a lesser woman. She lowered her voice to a pitch halfway between a whisper and a persuasive purr. "I've been thinking."

"What?" he asked, against his better judgment.

"Do you think Grace really appreciates that Waterford punch bowl?"

"What are you thinking, Lillian?"

"I was thinking, actually, I'd . . . hold on to it for a while."

Max took his elbows off the counter and turned full face toward his ex-aunt-in-law, where he'd have a better chance of dealing with her.

"It's been my experience," she said, touching his sleeve with her fingertips, "that there's nothing like a little competition to sharpen one's appreciation for a former . . . possession."

A warning light blinked on in Max's brain. This was some kind of female conversational thing. He was beginning to get a hang for recognizing them. Lillian wasn't talking about punch bowls.

He eyed her skeptically, wondering exactly what she *was* talking about. "What exactly are you talking about, Lillian?"

She smiled at him. "You're right, Max. There is an

emotional subtext here. How clever of you to understand that. You've come a long way."

A long way toward what?

"So," she continued, "as long as we understand each other, I thought I'd just keep the punch bowl for a bit. Don't you think?"

Max gave it a try, turning over the logic, searching for something that could be classified as an emotional subtext.

What he came up with was that Grace, according to Lillian's agenda, would start to covet the punch bowl, Max would continue to covet his wife, and Lillian would be mixing up rum punch in style for her next party.

What was wrong with this picture?

SIX

The party celebrating Edmund's bottle sale was officially limited to the Goodbodys and Grace, but Lillian had crashed it.

In a big way, Max noted. She was presiding over Grace's Waterford crystal punch bowl, ladling out rum punch into little silver cups, and generally holding sway over the proceedings in the late Martin Goodbody's Victorian parlor as if she were the designated hostess.

He had to admit it looked like she was filling an empty niche. Nobody else had done much of anything to prepare for either a party or the upcoming appraisal of the house and its contents. The antique furniture and the Oriental carpets were nice but didn't encourage party behavior, the background music was a classical radio station, and most of the windows were boarded up against burglars. Only Lillian could have pulled off a festive atmosphere, and she'd done it with typical aplomb.

He'd shown up for the proceedings wearing a white shirt and tie under his leather jacket, hoping to assail the respectable Goodbodys without raising too many eyebrows. As it happened, the company had been plied with enough of Lillian's punch to stave off any questions about party crashers.

Max strolled into the room, hands in his pockets, nodded to a solidly built woman standing beside Edmund and peering fuzzily at him, and put his hand out to take the little cup Lillian had just filled.

She blinked only once. "Why, Max. Don't you look lovely. I didn't know you owned a tie."

He grinned. "You like it?"

"Oh, absolutely." Her glance flicked down over him. "There's something about a black leather jacket and a tie that . . . speaks to a woman." She ran a burgundy-colored fingertip along the curve of her collarbone.

Max had a passing sympathetic thought for Ernie, which probably would have been more heartfelt if he hadn't caught sight of Grace glaring at him, an expression in her brown eyes that he'd have to say was outrage.

"What's the occasion?" Lillian asked.

"I thought I'd enter the estate market," Max told her.

"The *Goodbody* estate market?"

He smiled. "I'm trying to look like someone the Goodbodys would be nice to."

Lillian batted her eyelashes. "I'd be nice to you, Max, dressed like that."

Out of the corner of his eye he saw one of the Goodbodys—the woman who'd stared at him—moving toward them, determined snobbishness in her eye and Edmund in her wake. Grace had crossed her arms in front of her, one hand gripping her punch cup, which was tilting dangerously. Outrage, Max noted, wasn't exactly the expression on her face now. Or maybe it was, but there was something essentially female about it. He didn't know what could be particularly female about outrage, but there was a sort of spark . . .

"Max," Lillian said, putting her hand on his sleeve, "this is Marian Goodbody."

Max wrenched his gaze away from Grace and turned toward Marian. She had to be Edmund's mother. She looked just like him. Well-groomed, securely stocked and bonded, and with a lot of rectitude. If she stood up any straighter, she'd probably tip over backward.

"I believe," Lillian added, "you've already met Edmund."

Max nodded.

"Ah," Edmund said, as if he knew something. "You're Lillian's . . . friend."

Max raised an eyebrow at him, but was distracted by the sight of Grace setting her punch cup down on an end table. Amazing that she hit it, he mused, since her gaze was glued to his face and her expression was now close to murderous. Definitely more than outrage, he decided. She looked . . . like a woman on the warpath. Fired up. Determined. Passionate. God, when Grace was passionate, she was . . .

"Max is a collector," Edmund explained to his mother. He turned back to Max. "Are you interested in buying from the estate?"

"You might say that," Max said.

From the opposite corner of the room, a wiry, gray-haired woman in running shoes—she had to be Eloise—was converging on the small party gathered around the punch bowl. Grace had taken a deep breath and raised her chin.

"Max is an *avid* collector," Lillian cooed, linking her arm through his.

"Is he, now?" said Eloise.

"Oh? He is?" said Marian.

Truth to tell, no answer seemed necessary. The members of the assembled party were assuming convenient interpretations with no help whatsoever from Max. Reeboks was summing him up with raised eyebrows, Marian was giving him the pass-or-fail eye, and Lillian was leaning toward him and sighing happily.

Grace, moreover, was making tracks toward the action, which, Max had to admit in all modesty, was him.

"Of course he's a collector, Marian," Eloise snapped. "The question is, what's he collecting?"

Marian bristled. "I think *I* would be in a better position than you to answer that question, Eloise, as it pertains to Martin's estate. After all, Martin was my brother."

Eloise snorted. "The only thing you and Martin had in common was hemorrhoids. And Martin at least had a sense of humor about them."

"Aunt Eloise. Mother," Edmund said. Nobody acknowledged him, which, Max decided, wasn't surprising. The man might be respectable as hell, but he had all the authority of a traffic cop at a rock fest. Set up between Marian and Eloise, the most intelligent thing he could do was duck, but since he didn't seem to be smart enough for that, Max wasn't going to bother pointing it out.

His attention, in fact, was still on Grace, who was still staring at him, her gaze shooting daggers. She was that miffed that he'd shown up at the party? He'd dressed for it, for Pete's sake.

"Mother, Aunt Eloise," Edmund said again. "The first step is for Grace and myself to appraise the estate. We don't even have an idea of the catalog yet. But with the two of us working together—"

"Together?" Max interrupted.

"You're absolutely right, Edmund," Marian agreed. "I'll meet you tomorrow afternoon and we'll begin with the lower rooms."

"Not." Eloise planted her running shoes on the carpet and her hands on her hips. "We'll start by bringing everything down from the attic. And we might as well get going early in the morning."

"Eloise, if you think—"

"Mother—"

"Damn right I think."

"Eloise—"

"I might ask you the same question," Grace said to Max.

"Who, me?"

"Whoops," Lillian said, throwing out a hip and

connecting squarely with the punch bowl. The potential argument was sidetracked by a clinking of ice cubes and the bright smile on Lillian's face. "I have an idea," she said into the silence. "Why don't we all move in here, so we can appraise the estate together?"

The silence took on a stunned, confused quality.

Lillian waved a hand in an airy gesture. "I'll act as hostess, so the rest of you can get on with business. I did at one time live here, you know. A few dustcovers removed, a few supplies ordered . . . I can handle it."

"What'll we live on?" Eloise muttered. "Party crackers and rum?"

"But Lillian," Edmund said, "the house has been closed up for six weeks. The gas has been shut off, the windows are all boarded up, the—the water pump is turned off . . ."

Lillian beamed, set down her silver cup, and patted Max's arm with the hand that wasn't already looped through his elbow. "Not a problem," she said. "Nothing at all for a handyman."

"But we don't *have* a handyman, Aunt Lillian," Grace said, suspicion in her voice.

"Oh, don't worry, Grace," Lillian tossed out. "Max can take care of all that."

"Huh?" Max said.

Standing on the sidewalk, Grace reached into the back of her car, snagged a can of soda from the six-pack on the seat, and popped the top.

She needed something to cool her off, and one

mouthful of Aunt Lillian's rum punch had probably exceeded her limit on alcohol—not to mention her limit on shameless duplicity.

Lillian and Max?

Grace took a long swallow.

The rest of the party had been so busy mentally speculating on Lillian's relationship with Max that Grace doubted anyone had noticed her leaving. Two seconds after that thought formed, though, the front door of the house opened again, and Max walked out of it.

Grace ignored him as he strolled down the front steps and across the lawn toward the street. It was an immutable fact of life, however, that it was nearly impossible not to choke on one's soda when trying to drink it under your ex-husband's scrutiny.

"You got another one of those?" he asked her.

She shrugged. "Help yourself."

He leaned through the window of her car to get himself a can. "Thanks. I'm not sure what Lillian was trying to do with that rum concoction. Sterilize the punch bowl, maybe."

"Oh, I think she has something more in mind than killing bacteria."

"She usually does."

Grace gave him a disgusted look. He frowned back at her.

"So," she said, before he could speak, "are you working for Aunt Lillian again?"

"No. I'm still working for you."

"You're working for *me*, with that little charade in there?"

"You asked me to check out Lillian, right?"

"I asked you to see what she was up to, Max, not move in with her!"

"Move in with her?"

"This whole ridiculous idea! We're all going to move into Martin's house together to appraise the estate? It's crazy."

"It's not crazy." He read her face and tipped his head to one side. "All right, so it is crazy. But think about it. The estate lawyer would probably agree with me. Marian doesn't trust Eloise. Eloise doesn't trust Marian. Nobody trusts Edmund. The only way you're going to get your job done is by letting them all keep an eye on each other while you do it."

"While *I* do it. With Lillian pretending to be a chaperon and *you* pretending to be some kind of handyman-boyfriend."

"Is it so unthinkable that—" He stopped, blinked, then shook his head as if clearing the brain cells. "Handyman-*what*?"

"It's a little late for the innocent act, Max, when you've been playing *guilty* so well."

"Wait a minute. You think that Lillian and—and *me*?"

"No, of course I don't. But everyone in the Goodbody family does."

"Oh?"

Grace stared at him. That *oh* had a question mark at

the end of it, as if he were just now considering the possibilities implied here, and they looked like they had . . . possibilities. "Gracie? Are you jealous?" He actually appeared pleased with the prospect.

"What? Of Lillian?" she snapped, expelling a breath of exaggerated disbelief.

"No. Of me." This time he actually beamed, the happy bone of contention.

"That is the most egocentric, male-logic-ridden, testosterone-twisted, preposterous—"

"Yeah. Maybe it tells you something, Gracie."

Oh, it did, Grace decided. It told her she should have had more of Lillian's punch. If she weren't pregnant, she'd march back in there and fill up a beer stein with it. "*What*, exactly, is it supposed to tell me?"

"That you're jealous."

"Oh?"

"Yeah. About us. You and me."

"I am not—" She broke off, took another swig of soda, and partially crushed the can in a jealous pique. "Oh, all right," she snapped. "I'm jealous. So what?"

"So what?"

"Yes. So what? So I haven't quite risen above all my lower emotions."

"*Lower emotions?*"

She flicked him a glance. "I admit there's a certain animal attraction between us, Max."

"*Animal* attraction?" His enjoyment of the situation waned before her very eyes, eliciting a niggling spurt of guilt in Grace. She knew very well that she'd been pulling a Lillian and enjoying it. "*Animal attraction?*" he said again, sounding hurt.

"What?" She swirled the soda in her can. "Lillian's the only woman who can feel animal attraction for a man? I'm just suddenly too domestic to feel anything like animal attraction?"

Max's brow furrowed.

"I should just get in my minivan and go mow a lawn or something, is that it?"

"What minivan?" he asked.

"Oh, for Pete's sake, Max, it's a figure of speech."

"A figure of whose speech? Does this Edmund character have a minivan?"

"What?"

"Because, let me tell you, babe, he's not the only one."

Grace stared at him, dumbfounded by the leap of logic.

"You don't think I can handle a minivan?" Max asked her. "Let me tell you something. One week from today, tops, you're going to be looking at the minivan king."

"I am?"

"If I'm going to be the handyman around this place, I'm going to need a minivan."

"Max, for Pete's sake, you don't need a minivan!"

"Yeah? Well, I just might need one in the future."

In the beat of silence that followed, Grace stared at her husband, her eyes wide.

"You might as well admit it, Grace."

She crushed her soda can the rest of the way.

"Grace," he said, taking her arm, giving her the full benefit of his persuasive blue gaze, a man in charge of his fate and a step ahead of the prevailing logic. "This isn't about minivans. It's about . . . some kind of emotional subtext. I know the score on that . . . ah, score."

Emotional subtext? Was this Max she was talking to, discussing subtleties in psychobabble and claiming to know the score behind the minivan?

She took a breath. "Max," she said finally, her voice shaky, "I'm afraid you haven't got the whole . . . text, exactly."

"What? You mean about moving in here? Being a handyman? Fixing up old stuff when it breaks? Look, Gracie, maybe I haven't been all that handy in the past, but, hey, I can learn. Mowing the lawn, fixing the boiler . . ."

"This house doesn't have a boiler."

"Whatever." His hand tightened on her arm. "I can do it. How hard can it be, all that domestic stuff? I can handle it. Lawns, minivans . . . whatever turns you on, Gracie."

Grace stared into his sincere eyes and felt an iron band of emotion squeeze tight around her chest, a band made of intertwined strands of longing, hope, and fear.

"Max, you can't just reinvent yourself to be whatever turns me on."

"Why not?" He studied her, his eyes gradually darkening in a way that never failed to bring a little rush of heat in response.

And with the heat came that panic. She wanted this too much. She wanted *Max* too much.

"Be-because," she stammered, "sooner or later you'll uninvent yourself, and you'll get tired of lawn mowers and—and tricycles, and you'll decide all this domesticity is just a drag on your lifestyle and you'll go trotting off to Asia or somewhere and just . . . dump me with Aunt Lillian! That's why!"

He looked perplexed. "What are you talking about? Trotting off to Asia? Dumping you with Lillian? You talking about your parents?"

"Oh, Max—" She half turned away from him.

He gripped her by the shoulders and turned her back. "No. Wait a minute. Does this have something to do with that role-model hang-up you mentioned the other day outside the police station? Something to do with, you know, the women in your family not having babies? Is that what this is about?"

"I don't—"

"*Why* are you talking about your parents, Gracie?"

"I don't know!" She wrenched herself away from him. "Yes, I do know. No, I don't. Dammit!" She flung the crumpled soda can into the backseat of her car and crossed her arms in front of her, confronting Max with belligerently raised chin and stormy expression. "I was perfectly clear on all this before you came trotting back into my life and pinging my punch bowl, Max! Now—now I don't know what I want! I can't make a simple decision. I don't know what's the matter with me! I can't even define my problem!"

Max studied her, started to speak, then stopped,

rolled his shoulders inside the leather jacket, and shifted his weight to one foot and back again.

"Well, Gracie," he said, crinkling his eyes. "Did you ever have the thought that maybe, you know, just an odd possibility, kind of, that maybe . . . you're pregnant?"

SEVEN

"Congratulations," Ernie said.

Max glowered at him from the other side of Ernie's desk in the station room. "That's all you've got to say? My wife won't speak to me, she's about to move in with some bozo who's the executor of the estate, I still don't know whether I'm going to have a baby or not, and all you can say is, *Congratulations*?"

Ernie reached for a doughnut. "It's been—what? Two months? Trust me, Max. That's long enough to know whether you're going to have a baby."

"No," Max said. "No, this can't be so."

Ernie shrugged. "Oh, yeah, it could. It definitely could. Matter of fact, it almost certainly is." He grinned. "Maybe you should see an obstetrician. First trimester, you know? You gotta take care of yourself."

Max squeezed his eyes shut, wrestling with opposing urges to strangle Ernie or to storm into Grace's doctor's office and demand answers.

"Let's see," Ernie muttered, chewing. "First trimester. Must be starting to form fingers and toes, probably sucking its tiny little thumb, having little baby thoughts . . ."

An inarticulate sound got stuck in Max's throat. He clubbed himself in the chest to get his lungs working again.

"Heart attack?" Ernie asked.

"For God's sake, Ernie, what does a guy have to do to get some understanding around here?"

"Understanding," Ernie said musingly, trying out the concept. "Let's see. You figure out, after a couple months apart, that your wife's going to have a baby. You get her talking about her anxieties and fears, and then you tell her that her problem is she's pregnant." He sucked some chocolate frosting off his teeth. "Tell you the truth, Max, understanding's kind of a reach."

"It came as a shock, Ernie. It just doesn't seem . . . real."

Ernie's handcuffs clinked.

"Look." Max tried again. "She didn't give me a chance to even think about it. She just charged back up the walk to the house, told me she wasn't discussing it, and if I brought up the subject in front of the Goodbodys she'd dump Lillian's punch over my head."

"Probably wouldn't have been fatal."

"Are you kidding? That stuff was about two thousand proof."

"Mm." Ernie sounded speculative, a man trying to decide if this was a case where capital punishment might have been justified.

"I didn't have a *chance* to bring up the subject, anyway. She wouldn't even speak to me, she was so busy schmoozing with the Goodbodys."

Ernie reached for another doughnut. "So they're all moving into Martin's house together?"

"Yeah," Max muttered. Momentary gloom dominated the conversation. "God," he went on, "I should have figured it out when she started talking about the minivan and the tricycles. And then after we broke into Lillian's, and she was talking about domestic role models and how the women in her family don't have babies."

"Obviously some of them do," Ernie said.

"Yeah." Max looked up at him. "That's what *I* said."

"And it didn't occur to you that Grace might be having a baby?"

"Not until she started talking about me eventually getting tired of tricycles and domesticity and dumping her with Aunt Lillian like her parents did when they got tired of domesticity."

"Grace thinks you're going to dump her with Lillian? Has she been working too hard?"

"I don't know." Max sat up straighter. "You think she's been working too hard? With this appraisal and everything? Isn't she supposed to be taking it easy?"

"No problem. Long as she doesn't lift any heavy furniture. But then, she's got Edmund to help with that, doesn't she?"

"Edmund?" Max coughed in contempt, then hit himself in the chest again. Heart attack, nothing. This was police brutality. He would swear Ernie was getting a sadistic charge out of this while he stuffed himself with chocolate-covered pastry. "*Edmund?* That bozo has all he can do to lift a checkbook."

"Mm," Ernie said. "Well, there's Marian and Eloise."

Max snorted. "Marian wouldn't even think about it. Eloise would probably try anything, but she can't weigh more than eighty-five pounds herself."

"No help there, huh? Well, I wouldn't worry about it. Gracie can always hire a good handyman if she—"

"No possible way, pal," Max interrupted. "She's got a handyman already, and you're looking at him."

"You?" Ernie said, raising his eyebrows.

"Yeah, me."

"Huh. Get yourself a hand truck, a couple of protective quilts, I guess you could do the job."

"Yeah. That's what I was thinking. A hand truck. A couple of protective quilts."

"Couple of screwdrivers, maybe."

"Right. Couple of screwdrivers."

"Duct tape."

"Yeah. Duck tape."

"Anybody's ever taken care of a house, you find most problems can be solved with duct tape."

"Absolutely." Max nodded.

"Household problems, I mean. Not things like, you know, your wife having a baby."

Max glowered at him again. "Did I say that was a *problem*? Huh? Even once? Did I?"

"Not to me. 'Course since it doesn't seem real, I suppose it's not a problem."

Max pinched the bridge of his nose, squeezed his eyes shut, and gritted his teeth.

"You thought about a college fund yet?" Ernie asked.

Definitely, Max decided, he should have strangled Ernie while he still had the strength. "My problem," he said, grinding it out, "is that Grace won't speak to me."

"Can't say I blame her. Does sound like you might get another crack at it, though. Everybody's really planning to move into the house together?"

"That's right."

"Lillian's scheme? And she got 'em all to agree to it?"

"The punch was pretty potent."

"So are those Bennet women."

Max roused himself from his musings about Grace enough to consider Ernie's comment. He knew the other man admired Grace—that was one of the mitigating factors in Max's urge to strangle him—but putting Lillian in the same sentence sounded like Ernie had sampled some of Lillian's punch. Or maybe some of her chocolate.

"I wonder what she's up to," Ernie said. "Trying to pass you off as her latest."

"I couldn't tell you. It did get Grace's attention, though."

"Maybe it works two ways," Ernie mused. "Getting someone else's attention, you know?"

Max frowned, trying to gauge how much of Ernie's attention Lillian had captured.

"You suppose she has her eye on Edmund?" Ernie asked.

"*Edmund?*"

"He doesn't sound like her type, does he?"

"No."

"So what do you think?"

Max opened his mouth to speak, but stopped himself before he said anything.

What he thought was that Lillian had her eye on Ernie, and that it wouldn't be long before she had more than her eye on him. Ernie was primed for a fall, big-time, right into Lillian's potent, chocolate-baited clutches, and it sounded like Ernie was set to charge into the trap on his own. Just another poor moonstruck sucker felled by Lillian's punch.

Max ought to warn him.

That was what friends were for.

He probably would have, if it hadn't been for that crack about the college fund.

It was a fact of human nature that when an opportunity for payback was offered, no self-respecting male had any business passing it up.

Max's mouth curved up a little—small satisfaction for the wear and tear on his psyche Ernie had been dishing out, but hell, better than nothing—and he drew in a breath that almost expanded his lungs to normal capacity. "I just don't know what to think, Ernie," he said, getting up to go.

Ernie was on his own.

❦――――――❦

So far, so good, Grace thought, putting away the milk and the olives. The refrigerator had started when she turned the dial, the lights were on, and cold water came out of the kitchen faucet when she lifted the spigot arm. With her microwave and a cooler full of frozen food, they could make do.

Edmund, Marian, Eloise, and Lillian were arriving at noon. Grace planned to have the kitchen stocked and the plumbing checked before they got there. That collection of temperaments didn't need any frustrations to add to the fray.

Neither did hers, for that matter.

The jar of strawberry jam in her hand plunked down on the counter as she let her shoulders slump and stared bleakly at nothing.

The idea that Max thought she was a *problem* hurt too much to face straight on. She ought to feel justified, she told herself fiercely, clenching the jar in her hand. She'd been right. Max hadn't deserved to be told about the baby. Now that he'd figured it out, let him deal with the emotional implications on his own, the way she'd had to.

She hoped he was having a nervous breakdown. She was glad he was so confused by her *problem*. Good.

But she didn't feel good. She felt wretched. Wretched and lonely and abandoned. And she couldn't stop thinking about the times they'd been together, Max grinning at her when she woke him, reaching for her, lying about how soon they had to get up. Max coming into the kitchen with a bag of take-out food, suggesting they had better things to do than cook. Max leaning over her on the living room sofa, or the back-seat of his car, or his office swivel chair . . . Lillian's stairs . . . the back of the police station. . . .

The fact was, she hadn't gotten over him in two months. Max still made bells ring for her, even when he wasn't pinging her punch bowl. He still made her pulse quicken, her head feel light. He still made her feel sensual and beautiful and, yes, reckless.

And when he touched her, she just wanted . . . more.

She shut her eyes and rested her hands against the edge of the counter, giving in for a moment to the heady, sensual recollection of Max's touch, floating for just a few seconds into a realm of sweet fantasy, where Max became a gentle, reflective, understanding presence who'd reassure her and support her and be a strong, quiet, paternal force while she came to terms with—

Something struck the side of the house hard enough to rattle the toaster oven, and Grace jumped six inches off the floor.

She spun around toward the shrieking sound of nails being wrenched out of wood. A sliver of light appeared at the edge of one boarded-up window, then the plywood peeled down from the outside of the glass and crashed onto the lawn at Max's feet.

"Gracie?" he said, jiggling his hammer.

She wrestled open the window, willing her pulse to slow down and trying to catch her breath. "What are you doing, Max?"

"I thought you might be here. You know, working

early. Thought I'd get a start on uncovering some of these windows. Since I'm the handyman."

She stared at him, peered down at the rubble on the lawn, and said faintly, "I guess you've made a start, all right."

He looked down at it, too, then glanced up at her and grinned, apparently pleased with his progress.

He didn't look at all like he was having a nervous breakdown. He didn't even look as if he were dealing with emotional implications. He looked . . . She couldn't figure out how he looked. She wanted to strangle him and smile at him in almost equal measures.

"You have any coffee in there?" he asked.

"Instant," she said.

"Great." He waved at her with the hammer, then headed for the back porch. Grace stepped away from the window, leaned against the counter, and tried to prepare herself for another encounter with her ex.

There was no preparation for Max, though, she decided as he threw the back door open and walked through it. He'd caught her off guard, once again, surprised her with effects and realities she didn't want to face. She sighed, involuntarily seeking refuge in the fantasy Max had interrupted in a big way.

He was dressed, as usual, in white T-shirt and jeans, minus the leather jacket, but with a wide, heavy-duty leather tool belt slung around his lean hips, hanging low with the weight of a hammer, tape, pliers, wire clips, and a collection of shiny new screwdrivers. Never once, in their year of marriage, had she seen Max in a tool belt, and she knew he was no handyman, but for some reason the male accoutrements fit him as if they were made for him. For some reason, on Max, those screwdrivers looked potently, vitally, positively Freudian.

"You having trouble breathing?" he asked.

Grace gathered her scattered composure. "I was making . . . plans."

"Oh." He shifted his weight to one hip, propped his thumbs into the sides of his tool belt, and shrugged into a casual slouch, a consciously masculine posture that underscored a hint of uncertainty when he repeated, "Plans."

"Yes."

"You mean plans for the . . . ah . . ."

She blinked, realizing he was talking about the baby. Even if he couldn't quite bring himself to say the word.

She didn't feel like smiling. She didn't feel at all like smiling, she decided. But she didn't exactly feel like strangling him, either. Maybe, in fact, she felt like . . . talking to him.

"I was referring to the appraisal," she said finally. "I've already made plans for the . . . ah . . ."

He stood up a little straighter, nodding. "Yeah," he said. "Right."

She couldn't tell if he was relieved or disappointed that she'd diverted the subject away from her pregnancy. He was looking at her as if he wasn't quite sure what to make of her, studying her face for clues of change. When his gaze slipped down toward her stomach, she covered it with one hand—a classic prospective mother's gesture that, she realized, was becoming natural.

He drew in an audible breath, coughed once, and beat himself on the chest.

"Max? Are you all right?"

"Fine. Fine. No problem. No problem at all. Really, I mean that. No . . . ah, problem. This just seems kind of . . . unbelievable." He frowned. "Doesn't it?"

"I guess maybe that depends on what you believe, doesn't it?"

"Listen, Gracie," he said after a pause, "I figured out what you meant about the minivan. And the lawn mower. And—" He glanced away, then looked back at her. "I know I haven't been much of a domestic type of guy."

"Oh, Max . . ."

"But, really, babe, I might just—" He wrapped a hand around the handle of his hammer and jiggled it. "I might just have a knack for it, with a little practice." He waved a hand toward the window. "I mean, there wasn't that much to it. Couple yanks, pull a couple nails, came right off."

She looked toward the window, then back at her husband. Maybe he had meant that he really didn't believe it. He was acting pretty oblivious. "Max, there's more to being domestic than pulling boards off windows."

"Oh, I know." He clinked his tool belt and gave her a quick grin. "But with the right tools, maybe a handbook or two. And duck tape."

"Duct tape?"

"Duck tape. And, you know, if you need any help moving furniture or anything like that, I could . . . move some furniture for you."

She felt a momentary jolt of sensuality, a fleeting reference to Max talking about moving his bottles. She suppressed it, with a sigh. "Actually, I'd love to get started bringing things down from the attic, or out of the back rooms, but Eloise and Marian can't agree on where to start, so I'd probably better not disturb even the dustcovers until they're both here. With Edmund as a neutral witness."

"He's neutral, all right," Max muttered.

Grace frowned at him. Had he said "neutral" or "neuter"?

"And don't forget Lillian," he added.

"I'm not likely to. I know she's after something."

"Or someone."

"Someone?"

"Not me," Max said hastily, reading her mind. "I'm just the distraction."

"Oh." Her little flood of jealousy ebbed. "The distraction."

"Aren't you going to ask which third party I'm a distraction for?"

"I'm sure you're a distraction for quite a few third parties, Max."

"I am?"

Her gaze flickered, involuntarily, down over her husband's broad shoulders, muscled chest, lean belly, Freudian tool belt. When she looked up again, his eyes had gone dramatically dark, all intense and soulful.

A wash of heat rolled up from the center of her body in familiar, autonomic response.

"Yes," she admitted. "That's the problem, Max."

He didn't move, but she could sense his response as surely as if she'd hit him with a bucketful of cold water. "That's the *problem?*" he said. "What do you mean that's the problem? You mean that's . . . *the problem?*" His gaze flicked toward her waist.

"What are you talking about, Max?"

"Us. Making love all the time. When we are together. You mean that was what was responsible for . . . right?"

Grace frowned at him. Had she missed something in that question? "That *is* what's responsible for babies, Max. As you know. I think."

He shoved one hand back into his tool belt, agitated. "Of course I know, but—" He gestured at her. "But what you're saying is that we shouldn't have been together, or something. Like having that kind of sex was some kind of *problem*."

"I didn't say that."

"You didn't say anything, Gracie. You didn't tell me. Is that why? Is that why you—?" He broke off, gesturing again. "Well, why *didn't* you tell me?"

She'd had her reasons, Grace reminded herself. She took a guilty breath and lifted her chin. "I didn't tell you, Max, because I'm not *blaming* you for anything, okay? So you don't have to feel *responsible*."

"I don't?" His voice had gone from wounded to incredulous. He shifted his weight again, straightening up fast enough to make his screwdrivers rattle. "What's that mean? That I'm *not* responsible?"

"Oh, for Pete's sake," she muttered. She pushed herself away from the counter and stalked toward the door.

"Where are you going?"

"Out to my car to get the microwave. I need a cup of coffee."

He stalked after her and reached around her to pull open the front door. He held it for her, then remained a glowering presence beside her as she crossed the porch, the driveway, and the sidewalk to her car. He peered in the window, yanked open the back door of her car, then reared back again and fixed her with a disconcerted look. "That's not a microwave."

"No. It's an aquarium. I was going to have my neighbor feed Lucifer, but she's gone, and I didn't want to leave Lucifer on his own. The microwave's behind him."

Max scowled, then reached in past Lucifer and took out the microwave unit.

He gave her another angry glare as he stood up and pushed the door shut with his knee. "You were going to do this yourself?" he asked her.

"Yes. But thank you," she said.

"You don't have to thank me. I'm the handyman around here. I'm *responsible* for this sort of thing."

"Good," she said warily.

She opened the door for him, then followed him back into the kitchen. "I thought I'd put it beside the range, Max."

"Okay." He set his load down. "Is there a plug here?"

"Behind the bread box."

He checked. "Yeah. That should do it."

"Good."

"You have to have the right kind of plug, you know. A double outlet, since the toaster oven's already plugged in here."

"Oh. Double outlet."

He slanted her a slightly suspicious glance, as if he wasn't sure she was taking him seriously, then nodded and said, "Absolutely. You can't just plug these things in anywhere."

"As long as you can plug them in *somewhere*."

"Oh, yeah," he said, drawing out the words like a practiced electrician. "No problem." He plugged in the microwave, checked the appliances, and switched on the toaster oven for a test run.

The electric clock on the wall pinged, the lights went out, and the refrigerator stopped running. Max gave a small groan. Grace wasn't so restrained.

Even in the dark Max's shocked look was disapproving. "Jeez, Gracie. Where'd you pick up that kind of language?"

"From Lillian. When I was fifteen."

"You never used to use words like that when we were living together." He paused. "At least, not for swearing."

Grace felt heat in her face at the memory of exactly those times when she'd teased Max with her language.

Max hadn't been in the habit of talking about sex. He'd leaned more toward demonstrations.

Sweet chariot! That *was* the problem. She couldn't spend five minutes alone with her ex-husband in an intimately, if artificially, darkened kitchen, without forgetting everything but that feeling . . .

"I think," she said, carefully refraining from any more impolite language, "we'd better find the fuse box."

". . . The fuse box."

"It's probably in the basement."

The door to the cellar opened off the kitchen and led to what looked like a black hole. Max put an arm around her shoulders, pulled her back from the staircase, then flicked on his flashlight. A high-powered beam of light illuminated the wooden stairs.

"I'll go first," he said protectively. She almost expected him to add, *Stay close behind me.*

The instruction was unnecessary, however. She couldn't let Max go downstairs alone. He'd never find the fuse box.

"What's it look like?" he asked at the bottom of the stairs, flicking the flashlight beam around the cavernous basement.

"I don't know. A box, I guess. Square. On the wall, I think."

"Well, if it's the electrical station or whatever, it must be where all these wires come from." With the flashlight beam he followed the wiring along the top edge of the walls to one corner of the basement.

Impressed, Grace followed him toward the corner where, in fact, the wires all fed into a gray metal box.

"Not bad, Max," she murmured.

"Yeah. I guess this is it. The fuse box." He opened it. "Hm. This isn't bad. It's all marked down here." He held the light on the neatly labeled panel. "Living room, basement, hot tub. Ol' Martin had a hot tub?"

"Yes. It's out back."

Max glanced at her, then apparently thought better of continuing the subject. "Here we go. Kitchen."

He plucked out the little glass fuse, held it up in the beam of the flashlight, then, for reasons she couldn't ascertain, shook it beside his ear.

The house was so quiet, she could hear the soft rustle of his clothes, the faint clink of the flashlight against the door of the fuse box, all the deep vibrations in his voice when he said, "I think it must be blown. You know, when you blow a fuse."

"Mm. Must be. Are there any replacements lying around?"

He played the light over the immediate area. On a shelf next to the wall was a little cardboard box that proved to be full of replacement fuses.

"Pay dirt," he said. He stared into the box, shook it once, poked around the contents with his finger, then, on the wave of a brainstorm, produced the bad fuse he'd taken out of its socket and picked out a new one by comparison.

"Have you got the right kind?" Grace asked anxiously when he put the rest of the fuses back and, with what she would have classified as overconfidence, swung open the door to the electrical box.

"Sure. They both say twenty amps."

"What's that mean?"

"Got me."

"Max . . ."

"Hold this light on this thingy here, would you?"

She took it. "Max, do you think . . . ?"

"Hey, there you go."

Above them, light flooded down the stairway from the kitchen, and the refrigerator motor hummed emphatically into the silence.

"Oh," Grace said. She smiled. "You *did* it, Max."

"Well," he said modestly, "you held the light."

She laughed, half because it was funny and half because Max had taken back the flashlight, switched it off, and was grinning down at her, his expression in the dim light from the stairs smug and male. Any moment now it would dawn on him that if he was the defending man rescuing his household from the ravages of blown fuses, then she must be the grateful woman who would make it all worthwhile.

The idea had already, in fact, dawned on Grace, along with quite a few of those remembered images she'd been fighting in the kitchen. In the lengthening silence, those images became more vivid by the second, quickening her breathing and making her nervously aware that Max, too, was breathing faster.

"Actually," she said, glancing at the fuse box, trying for a normal tone, "I guess we could have just turned on the cellar lights. They'd be on a different fuse, wouldn't they?"

"Mm," Max said.

He wasn't thinking about fuses. She could tell, even in the near darkness, that he had images of his own scrolling through his mind. His grin faded slowly, and his eyes fixed on hers with an intensity she felt down to her toes.

"Gracie," he said softly.

"I guess . . . it would be . . . a different fuse, don't you . . . ?"

"Grace."

She didn't answer him, but she didn't stop looking at him either, and when he reached out and set the flashlight on top of the fuse box she felt her stomach catch.

He cupped her face in one hand, lowered his mouth to hers, and kissed her.

Not a gentle, tentative kiss. It was a passionate no-nonsense, take-no-prisoners kiss, with his mouth slanted on hers, moving against her lips until she opened them, and his tongue delving in to meet hers in one sweet, intimate, invasive shock.

His hands dropped from her face, and his body shifted as he bent his knees, lowering himself to her height, changing the angle of his mouth on hers. She felt his hands grip her upper arms, let go, grip again, as if he wasn't sure how much she'd permit.

She wasn't sure herself. Her heart hammered in all her pulse points, and awareness burgeoned up from deep inside her, running over her common sense like warm honey. Her own self-restraint vanished at the first sign that Max was exercising his. She rose up onto her toes, getting closer to him, making a soft, needful sound in the back of her throat.

He answered her with a sound of his own, and his hands left her arms to cup the back of her head, increasing the pressure of their mouths. She wrapped her own hands around his waist and cupped the ridged, muscled contours of his rib cage. Sliding her hands upward, around his back, she pulled herself closer, until she was pressed against him breast to chest, stomach to stomach, in a rough, impulsive embrace that felt so good, her heart leaped into faster rhythm.

At the waist of her jeans she felt the hard ridge of Max's zipper—and Max—pressed against her. When he moved his hips in a slow S, suggesting things, she hooked one leg around the back of his knees, a response that transcended thought. The sweet, graphic contact of their bodies made her gasp.

"Max . . ." she murmured.

"Oh, yeah," he murmured back. "You've got the right man, babe."

And the right man he was: solid, strong, passionate, purposeful.

"Max," she said again, against his lips.

"Mm."

Max? Oh, Maa—aax.

Max's mouth stopped moving.

Grace opened her eyes, then blinked in confusion. She hadn't said that last *Max.*

It had been an echo.

From the top of the cellar stairs.

In Aunt Lillian's voice.

She pulled away enough to break the contact of their kiss. Above them they heard the sound of Lillian's high heels trotting across the kitchen floor. "Max? Are you down here? In the basement?"

Max's hands curled around her shoulders. He lowered his mouth to her ear, and she had the distinct impression he was going to whisper *Don't answer*, in the vain but optimistic hope that Lillian would go away.

Grace knew better. Her aunt Lillian wasn't the going-away type. She'd flick on the cellar lights, come tripping down the stairs, and catch the two of them necking like a couple of teenagers in front of the fuse box.

"Down here, Aunt Lillian," she called. Max made a subaudible groan, a sound full of incipient pain.

"Grace? Are you in the cellar . . . with Max?"

"We were just changing a fuse, Aunt Lillian." She reached over Max's shoulder for the flashlight. "I was holding the light."

"Oh." It was a three-note word, up and down the scale, highly suggestive and, no doubt, in tune with Aunt Lillian's X-rated imagination.

Reality insinuated its way into Grace's consciousness like a pushy bottle buyer looking for a bargain. Flashlight or no flashlight, they'd been caught consorting, and no explanation was going to convince Lillian otherwise.

Probably, Grace thought as a little more reality niggled in, because there was no explanation. There never had been. Grace and Max, together, was a phenomenon that could not be explained.

"Well, don't let me interrupt you, then," Lillian said from the top of the stairs. "We do need our fuses, don't we?"

"No, it's all right. We're finished here," Grace called back.

"No, we're not," Max said in a low voice. "Not by a long shot."

"What does that mean?"

" 'A long shot'? Got me. But whatever it is, babe, we're not through by it."

Grace wasn't foolish enough to argue the point. Not with Max staring down at her with that intense blue gaze, his mouth set and quirked up at the corners, his expression knowing, masculine, and highly pleased with himself despite the interruption by Lillian.

She drew in a shaky breath, contemplating him, wondering if she should be worried and coming to conclusions she couldn't handle just yet.

Like what the smug expression was about. He looked as if he'd just proved something. She blinked again, trying to fend off those pesky conclusions. They didn't want to be fended, though. Adjectives were sashaying through her brain with abandon, and they all seemed to have a place in her unwilling self-examination: weak-willed, hormone-driven, utterly unable to resist Max Hogan whenever she let him get within touching distance of her.

"Why don't you have Max change the rest of the

fuses while he's at it?" Lillian suggested. "As long as you're down there with all that electricity."

She had that one right, Grace thought, feeling slightly desperate. There was enough electricity between her and her ex-husband to blow every fuse in her psyche. Maybe she already had. Maybe she'd been born with a genetically weak fuse system, and Max had been the catalyst to transform sensible, bookish, coolheaded Grace into a Lillianesque sexpot who melted every time he laid a hand on her.

She shuddered delicately, and felt herself swaying toward him, lured by his electricity, Lillian's outrageous suggestions, and her own burgeoning sensuality. She caught herself just as Max's hands slid down over her shoulders in a movement that was millimeters away from being a caress.

"No," she said, a blanket denial that she had to admit was mindless and all but meaningless.

"We could meet down here later, Gracie," he murmured, his voice raw and sexy enough to drive an electron crazy.

"No."

"Lillian doesn't have to find out."

"No."

"I could blow another fuse."

She groaned, squeezed her eyes shut, and made a protesting whimper in the back of her throat.

Max's hands stilled, the heat from his palms seeping into all the little nerve endings just under her skin. "Why not?" he asked. "We have a whole box of 'em here."

Grace got hold of herself and switched on the flashlight. Desperate to change the ambience, she followed the beam to the outlet box at the bottom of the stairs and flicked on the overhead fixture. Light flooded the stairwell, and Max coughed once in a reaction that sounded like some sort of allergy.

She ignored him and marched up the stairs to meet Lillian.

Her aunt was fiddling with the buttons on the microwave, holding a cup of water in one hand. Grace reached over her, punched the necessary buttons, and put the cup inside.

Lillian peered at her, eyebrows knitted, gaze discerning. "Where's Max?" she asked.

"He's still in the cellar."

One of Lillian's eyebrows rose. "Composing himself?" she asked archly.

Heat rushed into Grace's face. Maybe he was . . . composing himself. He hadn't, as she well knew, been in any state to meet company when they'd finished . . . consorting.

What was it with Lillian and her habit of interrupting them whenever they were consorting? Did Lillian have some sort of sex ESP? Was Grace on her wavelength?

Did she even want to think about the implications of that?

"I thought you were all arriving at noon, Aunt Lillian. Aren't you a little early?"

"I didn't want Eloise to get here first."

"What's Eloise got to do with when you get here?"

"I was afraid she might . . . start without me," Lillian said, waving a hand in unhelpful explanation. "She's so quick, with those damn running shoes."

"Quick at what?"

"Oh, you know. Scooting up to the attic and . . . such."

The microwave beeped, and Max appeared at the top of the cellar stairs. Lillian, typically, ignored the microwave. "Max," she cooed. "Nice tool belt."

"Mm," Max said. His glance strayed toward Grace. She glanced away, just in time to see, through the one unboarded kitchen window, a small red sports car park at the end of the driveway. Eloise Goodbody got out of it and slammed the door. She was wearing a backpack to go with her running shoes.

"It's Eloise," Grace said, frowning. "An hour and a half early, just like you, Aunt Lillian."

"Not quite, dear," Lillian said complacently. "I was an hour and thirty-five minutes early."

"And how early," Grace asked her, "are Marian and Edmund going to be?"

The microwave beeped again, and another car stopped beside Eloise's.

"Oh, I imagine they'll be right along," Lillian said. "In fact, here they are now, I believe."

All of them turned toward the window to see Edmund's Volvo pull up behind the sports car and Marian's Cadillac. Mother and son joined Eloise walking toward the door.

"What's that Tedsy's got in his hands?" Max muttered.

Lillian made a small, interested humming sound, then said, "Oh, my. It looks like a gift box of chocolates."

EIGHT

Max got a better grip on Lucifer's aquarium, made sure the fish hadn't sloshed out coming up the stairs, then knocked gently with the toe of his work boot on Grace's closed door.

Nothing happened except that the aquarium got about ten pounds heavier. "Grace?" he stage-whispered, glancing up and down the hall. He didn't see anyone in sight, but he wanted to maintain a little discretion, just in case Grace felt inclined to pick up where they'd left off in the cellar an hour earlier.

He didn't hear anything inside. He kicked at the door again, jostling the water in the tank, as well as his collection of screwdrivers, which had also gotten heavier during the trip up from the car. "Open up, Gracie. I've got the fish."

"Max? Is that you?" He heard scurrying from inside, then the door swung open.

"Oh, thanks, Max," Grace said. She peered into the water. "Are you all right, Lucifer?"

Was *Lucifer* all right? What about Max? He'd carried the damn five-gallon aquarium up two flights of stairs, moving more briskly than necessary because, truth to tell, impressing Grace with his prowess as a handyman seemed to have nice results.

This handyman stuff was no picnic, however. "Where do you want him?" he asked, staggering a little for effect.

"Oh—don't drop him. Over there on the bureau will do."

Max grunted, and crossed to the bureau, which had been cleared of everything but a glass dish holding a few chocolates.

He paused for a moment, staring at the candy and feeling a surge of irritation. What the hell? He'd been trudging up the stairs with a fish tank while Edmund Goodbody was plying his wife with chocolates? And one of them was half eaten!

He set the fish down and avoided squashing both candy and dish by a few millimeters, a dicey moral victory of decency over personal preference.

"Thank you, Max," Grace said, trailing him to the bureau and then ignoring him to crouch down and tap the side of the tank with one finger. "Is this all right, Lucifer?" she asked solicitously. "Would you rather be near the window? Or on the night table?"

"Well, hell, Gracie," Max grumbled, "maybe he'd just like me to carry him around for the next couple of hours while he makes up his mind."

Grace straightened and glanced around at him. "Oh, I do appreciate your bringing him up here, Max."

"Mm." He gazed at her, wondering if he should point out that there might be other ways of saying thank you.

"I wouldn't have asked," she went on, "if I didn't think it was necessary. But I'm a little worried about him. I don't think he's doing well. I didn't want to leave him too long on his own."

Max gave the fish another look and refrained from pointing out that Grace hadn't had any trouble leaving *Max* on his own a couple of months ago. "How do you know he's not doing well?"

"He's listless, and he's not eating his fish flakes."

Max squinted at the goldfish. "Maybe he's on strike. He wants to be back in that punch bowl, where he could get a little ping once in a while. You know, that . . . reaction he had when—"

"I know the reaction you're talking about. And you're wrong. Lucifer is *not* on strike."

"Mm," Max said, trying to interpret her resistance to his theory. It seemed clear to him. Lucifer was suffering from lack of sensual fulfillment. He could relate.

"Maybe he's sick of fish flakes. Try him with a couple of chocolates." He picked up the glass dish and almost succeeded in dumping Edmund's chocolate offerings into the water before Grace snatched the dish away from him.

"Max, for Pete's sake! Fish don't eat chocolate."

Max eyed Lucifer again. Maybe this one did. Hell, if you couldn't get sensual fulfillment one way, you learned to sublimate. "Listless, hell, Gracie. Look at him. That's not listlessness. It's determination. He's on strike. He wants his punch bowl."

Grace didn't answer him, but he noticed that a delicate blush was tinting her cheeks. No doubt she was remembering their physical encounter in her front hall over the punch bowl. Hell, *he* was remembering it, and he wouldn't be surprised if a delicate blush was tinting his own cheeks, along with a suddenly urgent desire to see just how much heat they could generate over this particular fish tank in the immediate future. "Gracie . . ." The word came out low and rough with need.

"Don't, Max." She held up one hand.

"Don't what?"

"Don't try to . . . distract me. Divert me. We're talking about Lucifer here."

"Lucifer?"

"Yes! Lucifer. My fish. I'm the one who takes care of him, Max. I have to make sure he gets what he needs. I'm not a single entity anymore. I have responsibilities. I'm a . . . package deal."

A charged silence, rife with implications that were heavy enough to rearrange neurons, precluded any immediate answer. Max's neurons were too busy scrambling around, desperately seeking purchase.

This was another one of those subtexts, he knew. She was talking about her baby.

She was talking about *his* baby, in fact.

The insight was accompanied by a shortness of breath. It was becoming familiar. Max gave himself a thump on the chest.

A brand-new life, who was maybe even right now sucking his thumb and thinking little baby thoughts. It was unbelievable. It was some kind of miraculous event, wasn't it? Like the fountain of youth, or aliens landing in Arizona.

Max made a special effort to fill his lungs before he keeled over. When his nieces and nephews had been conceived he'd thought it was cool, but it hadn't seemed particularly supernatural. This, though—Grace being pregnant—was so monumental, it was hard to take in and still keep breathing.

A package deal, as if there were two of her in one body—Gracie and some other tiny Gracie. Or a tiny Max.

"Max?" she said. "Are you all right? Do you need to sit down?"

"No, no. I'm fine."

"Maybe you shouldn't have carried that aquarium all the way up the stairs."

He gave a passing thought to the two flights of stairs, which he'd climbed carrying a fish tank. Grace had climbed them carrying a baby.

"Grace," he said, taking her arm and leading her toward the bed, "I think you need to sit down."

She sat without protest, though she was looking at him warily. He didn't let go of her arm.

"Tell me something, Gracie. How far along are you on this . . . package deal?"

"You mean the baby."

"Y—" He nodded and tried again. "Yeah. The b-baby."

"About three months."

"Three months." He nodded again, calmly, then squeezed his eyes shut. Three months. God, that was unbelievable. For the past three months he'd been tooling around doing detective work, completely unaware, while Grace had been performing miracles.

Or actually . . . *Three months?* The actual miracle, now that he thought about it, had been performed while they were still living together. Of course it had. He'd been there, for Pete's sake, present at the event. *Participating* in the event.

"This is unbelievable," he muttered.

"What is?"

"You and this . . . baby thing. I mean, have you really *thought* about this? No." He pinched the bridge of his nose. "Of course you've thought about it. You've been thinking about it for three months."

"Well, two months, actually, Max."

"Two months." He stared at her. "Wait a minute."

"What?"

"That means—Wait a minute. That night you came home and found me in the hot tub with the bimbo, you knew you were, like, pregnant, then?"

She nodded.

He looked away from her, stunned. "Oh, boy," he said softly.

"Max, I—I tried . . ."

He frowned at her. "And that whole time we were having that argument about marriage and responsibility and all that stuff, you knew you were . . ."

"Pregnant."

"Yeah."

"Maybe I should have told you, Max. I intended to. I had every intention, but I just . . . didn't know how you'd . . . feel about it."

Her voice was hesitant, tentative, and a little breathy, as if she, too, were having trouble with her lungs. Max felt a rush of panic. She *was* breathing, wasn't she? She was pregnant, for Pete's sake! She had to breathe regularly. She had to—

She let out a long sigh and he felt his anxiety wane, leaving him drained. God, he had to get a grip on himself. "This is unbelievable," he muttered again.

Grace made a little sound in the back of her throat. "Max," she said, exasperated, "that's not a *feeling*."

"It is too."

"No it's not. It's a judgment!"

"Well, then, how am I supposed to feel?"

"I don't know that you're *supposed* to feel anything."

She was looking at him with big brown eyes full of hurt. Another strand of emotion added itself to the knot in Max's gut. "How do you want me to feel, Gracie?"

"I can't just *tell* you that!"

"Why not?"

"Because you have to figure it out for yourself, that's why not! You have to figure out your own feelings about it."

He stared at her. "About the baby," he said. "About your being . . . p-pregnant."

She took a deep breath, which marginally eased his remaining anxieties about her immediate well-being, but didn't do much for the rest of his anxieties. Clearly this was another one of those test questions.

"Yes," she said. "About my being pregnant."

Max himself took a breath, then searched her face for a long few seconds. Gracie was pregnant. A slight flush still colored her cheeks. Her gaze held a flicker of vulnerability that caught at his emotions, but there was a glow of something else there too. Determination, he realized. A quiet, no-nonsense purpose. It was the kind of character trait that went with parenthood, he guessed, maybe the kind of thing you achieved after you got over the unbelievable part. A muscle in his cheek twitched. Grace had decided, months ago, that she was going to do whatever she had to do, keep up her business, deal with Lillian, dump the bimbo and the hot tub.

There was an earth-mother strength about this whole package deal that amazed him. She even looked different. More feminine. Womanly. Female.

He shook his head, sorting through the unfamiliar feelings in an attempt to untangle them. "Grace, you know," he said finally, gentling his hold on her arm, "this whole thing is just amazingly . . . sexy."

She stiffened, obviously startled. "It is?"

"Yeah. It is."

"No, it isn't."

"Come on, Grace. You don't think it's sexy?"

"No!" She pulled her arm away from him and turned more squarely toward the side of the bed, her carriage rigid, but then relented and glanced back at him. "At least," she said, "I didn't think so until you came around, bothering Lucifer."

"Yeah. But then—"

"No." She waved him silent. "All right, yes, maybe, but that's not the point. Having a baby is not supposed to be an orgy, Max. Pregnant women aren't *sexy.*"

"Well, no, I don't have a thing for pregnant women in particular. I mean, not *other* pregnant women. But *you*, Gracie . . ."

"Oh, Max."

He didn't think he'd quite gotten his point across, or that he quite knew what the point was, but the attempt seemed to be all right. Grace's eyes had gone dark and sympathetic, her mouth soft and vulnerable, and the expression he read on her face elicited in him a whole new gamut of sweet, new-sprung reactions in addition to the sexy ones.

He moved in a little closer, carefully, brushing his palm up her arm. He reached for her with his other hand but stopped short of touching her, uncertain as to whether she'd let him touch her, uncertain, for once, exactly how to do it.

She glanced self-consciously toward the hallway.

Max followed her gaze, getting her point. The house was full of Goodbodys moving in according to Marian's assigned room plans as modified by everybody else. He got up and closed the door, giving them privacy.

Grace didn't move, and he came back and sat down beside her. Putting his hands on her shoulders, he turned her toward him, then hesitated for the space of a heartbeat before he touched her face with the back of his knuckles, both hands.

It was different, touching her. More . . . amazing. That must be what she'd meant by the feelings part. Amazing Grace, he thought.

When he leaned toward her to kiss her, she leaned toward him. She tipped her head in the opposite way he was tipping his, and met his mouth with the same gentle pressure he exerted.

For the moment, it was enough, he thought, astounded. A backwash of feelings swirled through him, and he could imagine them swirling through Grace, carrying currents of emotion like shared electricity, real and laced with power, even if there wasn't any way to say it.

Hell, they had a way to say it. They'd always had a way to say it, without words, the best way, and they didn't need any punch bowl pinging to do it. They'd always talked by making love. All they needed was a little contact, a touch on the shoulder, a brush down Gracie's back, a subtle move to get in closer . . .

Someone knocked on the door.

Max threaded his fingers into his wife's hair and touched her lower lip with his tongue.

Someone knocked again.

Max tightened his hold on her and willed his extraneous senses into oblivion. It might have worked except that he was pretty sure Grace had heard the knocking too. She stopped kissing him and pulled her head back.

"Grace?" Edmund called through the door.

Grace moaned.

"Don't answer," Max murmured.

"Grace, do you need any help?"

She turned her head toward the door. "Just a minute, Edmund. I'm not dressed."

"Don't tell him that!" Max whispered in her ear. "Now he's going to be standing out there picturing you in your underwear!"

"Max, for Pete's sake—"

"What?"

"Just wondered if you needed any help moving in your things, Grace," Edmund said.

"Oh, thank you, Edmund. That's sweet of you."

"*Sweet* of you?" Max hissed.

"Max—"

"What?"

"Get in the closet."

"The *closet*?"

"Now!"

"Now? Are you kidding?"

"Don't clink your tool belt!"

"Gracie—"

She wasn't listening. Whatever nonverbal communication they'd established, the connections were slipping like worn-out lock picks. Max found himself in the closet with the door closed before he could marshal the argument to keep himself loose.

And he couldn't hear a damn thing through the solid two-inch panel. Well, he could hear a couple of damn things. Grace had apparently opened the door to Edmund and was speaking to him in an entirely too courteous tone. Edmund laughed—a polite, socially appropriate laugh that made Max's toes curl in contempt, then Grace said something else.

He was beginning to sweat, in more ways than one. And why not? His wife was flirting with some bozo who'd just been standing outside the door picturing her in her underwear, and Max was hiding in a *closet*?

He fumbled for the doorknob, found it, and got the door open just as Grace was closing hers.

"He's gone?" Max asked.

"Yes. And so are you."

"*Me?*"

"Hurry up! Before someone else comes along!"

"Who else are you expecting?"

She crossed her arms in front of her and stared at him, giving an uncertain flip of her head, but standing her ground. She wasn't expecting anyone, Max surmised, but that didn't really matter. Sometime during his closet stay, she'd decided she wasn't expecting anything further to happen between them. The mood, apparently, had been broken.

By Edmund.

"Are you saying," Max asked, "that you don't want anything to happen that might get back to Tedsy? What do you care?"

"Max—"

"Who the hell is Tedsy to you, anyway?"

"My *client*."

"Oh, your *client*."

"Yes! I'm running a business, Max. It's important to me, right now at this time in my life, that I'm successful at it. I have to consider that."

"Oh? That means you have to cozy up to Tedsy Goodbody? Jeez," he muttered, disgusted. "It sounded like you two were just having a lovely little tea party there at the door."

"Edmund and I have a business relationship. We're not having a tea party. As responsible adults—"

"Wait a minute. I heard him. Tedsy baby wasn't thinking about being responsible, Gracie, although maybe the *adult* part fits in, as in adult films '

"For Pete's sake, Max, don't you ever think about anything but sex?"

He made a wordless sound of disbelief and slapped one hand against the closet doorjamb. "What?" he said. "Just because I mentioned a little truth about Tedsy's real motives? Just because—" He slapped his hand again against the wooden molding, huffing at her, then straightened, dropped his hand, and faced her. His expression changed. "This is about the baby, right? This is about that . . . responsibility stuff, right?"

She raised an eyebrow, but didn't answer him.

"Okay, okay." He held out a hand. "I get this. I know what there is to think about. Like obstetricians and . . . college funds, right?"

"You've been thinking about college funds?"

His gaze slipped, one small, self-conscious mistake, but he managed to catch it, look back at her, and shrug one shoulder in casual indication that finances were a day-to-day consideration for him.

"College funds?" she repeated.

"Well, not just now. Not when we were getting it on."

Grace seemed to choke. "Is that what we were do-ing?" she asked. "Is that what you think you were—"

"Ah . . . no. No," he said. "Not in so many words. I didn't actually mean it like—"

"Yes, you did."

"Gracie—"

"No, it's all right, Max," she said, sounding guilty. "You're right. That is what we were doing. And it was just inexcusable for someone like me. When I'm sup-posed to be here working, and I haven't told anybody I'm still married. Oh, Lord. I'm supposed to be a pro-fessional woman, and here I am, being irresponsible—"

Maybe he was the one who'd gotten into the guilty thing, Max thought. Whatever that emotion was, twist-ing through his insides, it was strong enough to carry the threat of terror in its wake. "Oh, Gracie, now, come on. Don't say that." He took a step toward her, reach-ing for her.

She backed away. "Don't start, Max. I just can't trust myself when you start things. And I can't *be* like that," she said, sounding a little terrified herself. "I'm going to be a parent."

"Yeah? And what about me?" He took another step toward her. "I'm going to be a parent too."

She wrapped her arms around herself and kept backing up, moving, Max thought, onto decidedly shaky ground. "I'm not asking you to do this, Max. To think about college funds. I'm not going to force you into being a responsible—"

"Why not?" he demanded. "You think I can't han-dle it?"

"No, I—I just . . ."

"Just because you think I'm not the responsible type, like Tedsy? Just because I don't walk around in a suit and make polite requests to somebody else's wife to help her move in?"

"He doesn't know I'm somebody else's wife, Max!"

"Then why don't you tell him?"

"It's a little late now. I just never did. It just didn't come up."

Max huffed again as words failed him.

"We have a *business* relationship, Max! We didn't discuss our personal lives, all right?"

"*Yet,*" he said.

"We're not going to, either! We have a business relationship, we keep our distance, and we don't think about sex all the time, because as a responsible adult, Edmund Goodbody has some restraint!"

Max reeled back as if he'd been slapped. "That's low, Gracie," he said on a strained breath.

She looked stricken. "I told you it wasn't entirely your fault. I admit some of the fault is—"

"No." He stopped her, holding up one hand. "I want to tell you, Gracie, I've got just as much *restraint* as all the Goodbodys put together, including Tedsy. You think I can't handle a little restraint? You think I can't do it? Just watch me, babe."

"Max—"

"No," he said again. "We don't have to discuss it. I'm going to walk out of here without touching you, Gracie. Not a hand. Not a finger. Not so much as an innuendo. You know why?"

"Why?" she asked faintly.

"Because I have restraint."

He left her with her mouth slightly open, her expression perplexed, her arms slipping down from their tightly crossed position, her eyes soft.

Brown and soft and accessible, Max decided as he pulled the door shut.

He stared at the wooden panels for a moment, feeling that funny, unwelcome shift in his gut that told him his emotions were resorting themselves and coming up, as usual, with surprises.

Had he been, maybe, too hasty?

Those eyes of hers, that sweet, vulnerable expression, the way she'd caught her lip between her teeth . . . Maybe he should have stayed a bit longer?

He let out an exasperated breath.

No. He could do this. He was going to be a parent. The thought didn't even make him sweat. Much.

Restraint. How hard could it be? If Grace wanted to keep her relationship with Edmund strictly professional by not telling him anything, Max could go along with that. Hell, he was going to be a parent. He could have restraint. All he had to do was not touch her. Not look at her too often. Not think about her more than once every five minutes.

No problem. He'd just stay at the other end of the house. He'd do his handyman gig and deal with Lillian and company and just keep at least one wing of the house between himself and his ex-wife and—

"Maxwell?"

"Huh?" he said, turning to see Marian advancing on him.

"I'm glad to find you at . . . ah, this end of the house," she said.

"You are?"

"Yes," Marian said crisply. "Now, Maxwell, I know that Lillian drew up a room plan and located you in the south wing."

"She did?" Max said, trying to figure out what the hell Marian was talking about.

"But in the interest of *propriety*—"

She said the word as if she were making a recording for the *Oxford English Dictionary*.

"—we all agree that you and Lillian should be at opposite ends of the house."

"Propriety," Max repeated.

"Yes. So we're putting you here."

"Here?"

"In the next room actually." She indicated the bedroom door fifteen feet down the hall.

"*Here?*" Max said again, beginning to sweat.

"I'm sure you'll be quite comfortable."

NINE

At 3:15 A.M. Grace admitted the truth of a troubling natural law: There was only so much restraint between Max and herself, and Max had appropriated all of it.

She pounded her pillow and stared at the sliver of light under her door. She had determined three hours earlier that it came from the lamp in Max's room, via the hallway. He'd left his door open, as if he were planning to slip into her room any moment now, but he hadn't made a move toward her room since he'd gone to bed.

He was reading. Every once in a while she could hear the rustle of a page being turned. At uneven intervals he'd scrunch around on the mattress, pound his pillow, rearrange the blankets, sigh a couple of times, and go back to reading.

Grace herself had spent the past three hours warding off heated fantasies of Max striding into her room, tearing off the covers, and sweeping her into his arms. None of those ideas, apparently, had occurred to Max.

Sometime before midnight he'd dropped his tool belt, climbed under the covers, and immersed himself in the pages of a good book. He hadn't so much as clinked a screwdriver since then.

And she wished he would, she admitted, feeling a jolt of desire that made her clutch the pillow to her chest. It wasn't much of a substitute for Max. But it had to be better than a book, didn't it? She drew in a fold of the blanket as well, clutching tighter, trying to ignore the fact that something squishy and inanimate had absolutely nothing to offer a woman who'd spent three hours imagining in vivid detail the sensory stimulation embodied in Max Hogan.

Grace sighed, rolled onto her back, and stared into the dark above her head. It must be a hormonal thing, something to do with pregnancy. One of those odd cravings like ice cream or olives or—or chocolate.

Chocolate. The imagined taste of it on her tongue diverted her for two and a half seconds from the thought of Max. But she'd already eaten all the chocolates on her dresser. She hadn't been able to resist them, in fact.

She might as well admit it. Along with Aunt Lillian's looks, she'd inherited her aunt's sensual nature. And Max had been her sensual equal, her nemesis, maybe. He'd brought her out of Lillian's exotic shadow, made her feel beautiful and exciting and . . . loved. And she'd missed him.

She missed him now.

Seeing him again, being with him, had stirred up all the needs and feelings she'd put aside in her first over-whelming reaction of panic.

Normal panic, her obstetrician had told her. Many new mothers felt some panic. It was a momentous tran-sition, and all kinds of emotional reactions were to be expected. Talk to her husband about it, the doctor had advised. *Talk to* had been the words, Grace reminded herself. Not *make love to*.

But then, her obstetrician hadn't met Max.

Another page turned, and Max went through the mattress-scrunching, pillow-pounding, sighing routine, but fifty sheep later—Grace was counting—he hadn't yet turned another page. At sixty sheep, she opened her eyes and hitched up on her elbows. Finally she heard the faint creak of bedsprings, another sudden silence, then, abruptly, the light went out.

Grace blinked, staring at the crack under her door, which was now dark. Quite clearly, she heard Max get out of bed. Cautiously, quietly, but definitely. Her heart started to pound.

Was he walking across the carpet? Bare feet crossing the floor? His door had been open all night, but she was sure she heard the faint creak of it being closed.

The little thrill of panic she'd felt earlier returned in force, brought on by some other emotion entirely. "No," she said to herself, rehearsing the word.

Max's nearly silent footsteps sounded in the hall-way, moving, she realized, away from her room.

"No," she said again, more sincerely, frowning at the door. The bathroom was the other way, past her room. Max was headed for the stairway at the end of the hall.

What was he doing? Going down to the kitchen for milk and cookies?

She slipped out of bed, crossed her room, and let herself out into the darkened hall, then paused long enough to give him a good head start. She didn't want him to think she'd been lying awake listening to him read. He'd probably make something of it.

When she was sure he'd gone downstairs, she slipped into his room. Her curiosity had been honed to a lethal edge in the past three hours. What, exactly, had Max Hogan been reading that was so engrossing he hadn't so much as twitched a toe outside his own covers?

She snapped on the light.

Baby and Child Care was lying facedown on the bed. He'd gotten about halfway through it, up to the chapter on middle-of-the-night feedings.

Grace stared at the book, incredulous. She'd been tossing and turning, wishing and hoping, tormented and burning for Max, while he'd been reading about burping techniques and midnight feedings?

Must have given him ideas about milk and cookies, she decided, her mouth quirked.

Either that, or he'd had an irresistible desire to rush out and start a college fund.

Max's burning desires of the moment had to do with where he'd left his lock picks, and his own curiosity was focused on the question of who had sneaked up into the attic in the middle of the night and locked the door.

Could have been any of the Goodbodys, he concluded, fishing a Swiss army knife out of his back pocket. They were all crazier than bedbugs.

He sprayed the lock with WD-40—one of the few handyman's aids he'd been familiar with for years—applied the toothpick from his knife, and let himself silently into the attic staircase.

It wasn't hard to locate the source of the sound he thought he'd heard. Someone up there had a light on, and about halfway up the stairs he could make out a quiet, rhythmic, squishy sound. Someone chewing on chicken legs? Molding mud pies? Wielding a paintbrush, methodically and single-mindedly?

He was right the third time. Lillian was standing in front of an easel, slathering black paint on what looked to be an already completed canvas.

He stepped on a tube of something that squirted underfoot. Glancing down at the spray of black paint on the floor, he swore with feeling.

"Max!" Lillian said, aggrieved. "Look what you made me do, for heaven's sake." She pinned him with a dissatisfied glare as she reached for a roll of paper towels. She dabbed at the painting, wiping off a streak of black from the background, which depicted a voluptuously appointed red and gold Victorian parlor.

The foreground, as clearly as Max could make out, was an equally voluptuous female figure reclining on a couch, but both figure and couch were shrouded in some sort of black drapery—*fresh* black drapery. The nude was wearing a hat with a veil that obscured not only her face but her body.

"What is it?" Max muttered, picking up the tube of paint. *Anonymous Black*, the label said. "More to the point," he said, moving in for a closer look, "*who* is it?"

Lillian stepped back from the painting to eye it critically. "I call it 'Mourning Lover,' " she said.

Max helped himself to a wad of paper towels, dipped it into the bucket of water by the easel, and wiped off a swath of *Anonymous Black*.

What appeared under the veil was a pair of soft brown eyes, delicately fair skin, pearlescent shoulders. He kept wiping. Graceful throat, voluptuous torso . . .

Max banged himself in the chest with the soggy paper towels, dampening his T-shirt. "Gracie," he breathed. "Oh my God."

"Grace?" Lillian repeated. She frowned, examining the painting. "Mm," she said finally. "I suppose there is a resemblance."

A resemblance. Max staggered backward and collapsed into a sheet-covered chair. The nude was Lillian, of course, but his vital functions were only just now absorbing that fact.

"Yes," Lillian continued analytically. "Grace does have the Bennet eyes, the Bennet chin."

Max gave her a shell-shocked look. The chin hadn't struck him, particularly.

". . . The Bennet collarbones. The Bennet . . ." She gestured with the brush.

Max beat himself on the chest again, splattering black paint over his T-shirt.

"What's the matter, Max?" Lillian asked, raising one shoulder sinuously. "You can't handle the idea that Grace might have had an interesting past?"

"Hmmph," Max managed.

"I thought men liked women of mystery."

"She has an interesting *present*, Lillian. She's pregnant."

"So was Demi Moore. That doesn't mean a woman has to completely give up her—"

"Stop, Lillian. Right there. With Demi Moore, you know?"

"Good heavens, Max. When did you become so conservative?"

"Parenthood does that for you."

"It does? Whyever should it? Besides, you didn't seem all that conservative when you and Grace were carrying on down by the fuse box."

Down by the fuse box? It sounded like the refrain of an old rock-and-roll song. "Lillian," he said, "why are you up here in Martin Goodbody's attic defacing this painting?"

"Defacing?" She stepped back a pace. "I thought it was quite an artistic effort. I always did have an artistic flair."

"I won't argue with that, Lillian. But why are you practicing it now?"

"Does there have to be a reason for art?"

"No. But there's usually a reason for graffiti."

"I *was* the model for this work, Max. That certainly

gives me some moral rights." She dabbed at the canvas, applying a stroke of black paint to replace part of what Max had wiped off.

"Lillian," he said, "I'm not sure what your moral rights are, but this probably isn't one of them. That painting is part of Martin's estate, isn't it?"

She glanced at him and drew in a deep breath, refusing to answer.

Max considered her reaction. "Wait a minute. Let me guess. For some reason Martin ended up with this painting when you divorced him, and you think it should have been yours."

"It certainly should have been mine."

"Uh-huh. And now that it's coming up for auction, you think you can . . ." He hesitated, perplexed. "I don't know. What? Sneak it out the back door?"

Lillian sniffed. "Of course not. Why would I want a stolen piece of artwork? I'd never be able to display it. I intend to buy it."

Max eyed her warily, then sighed, exasperated. "That's why you wanted Gracie to handle this estate? Because you wanted this painting?"

"Little good it did me. I brought up the subject in a general way. Grace won't *hear* of anything being sold privately. Not even within the family. Something about Martin's will specifying that everything be auctioned." She made another black slash. "*Public* auction, to make it worse. Perfect strangers *bidding* on items like this!"

"That's what an auction is, yeah."

"*I* could be outbid! I don't have unlimited resources, you know. What if there are museum representatives there? What about some wealthy private collector?"

Max raised his eyebrows. "Might be the start of a great relationship, Lillian."

"I am *past* the age of marrying for material gain, Maxwell. Any man who can't live without this painting will have to petition *me* for my hand, not the other way around."

"Petition," Max muttered. "Yeah." He rubbed his forehead. "Have you considered that Grace's professional reputation is at risk here, Lillian?"

"Oh, don't be so moralistic, Max. Grace doesn't even know about this."

"Yeah, but Lillian? As of now, *I* do."

Lillian frowned at him, paintbrush in hand, one eye on the partially defaced painting, the other assessing Max's loyalties and determining them to be a problem.

"Well," she said.

"Well?"

Lillian stopped frowning and gazed at him with the kind of cool assessment he'd seen before in her expression. "As you said, Max, one wouldn't want just *anyone* to have the pleasure of viewing the Bennet . . ."

She gestured with her brush. Max eyed both Lillian and the painting skeptically, ignoring the twist in his gut that had to do with the other female presence invoked by this insane conversation: Gracie.

"Edmund, for instance," Lillian went on. "One wouldn't want someone like Edmund to be *handling* an artistic work of this personal nature, now would one?"

Max shut his eyes and drew in the acrid air of *Anon-*

ymous Black and Lillian's insidious suggestions. She was playing off his jealousy, purely and simply, manipulating his emotions to suit her own agenda.

It was working too. One mention of Edmund and Max's green-eyed monsters not only sat up and took notice, they stomped on his chest, poked him in the gut, and trussed up his heart in its own strings.

Unfortunately, he was in a vulnerable state. He'd just spent three torturous hours thinking about his wife in the next room over and suffering throes of temptation and muscle spasms in delicate places. He'd gotten halfway through *Baby and Child Care* because that particular subject was the only thing that could keep him from ripping off the blankets, charging into her room, and forgetting the hell out of his restraint initiative.

The idea of Grace sleeping alone was bad enough. The suggestion of Grace being fantasized about by someone like Tedsy was enough to push him over the edge.

"The main thing," Lillian continued, "is that we both have Grace's interest at heart, don't we, Max? I mean, absolutely the most discreet thing would be to keep this personal little secret in the family, don't you think?"

He dragged his fingers down his face and propped his chin in his palm. "Absolutely the most discreet," he said. He could feel himself slipping and sliding down the primrose path of discretion with every passing brush stroke.

"I think it's just charming that you're adopting

these family values, now that you're going to be a father, Max."

He eyed her skeptically. Even Lillian couldn't believe that lying to one's spouse and participating in an auction scam constituted a family value.

"Discretion is sometimes the better part of valor, Max," she went on persuasively. "You wouldn't want to rock the boat right now, would you, with things between you and Grace in such a state of . . . mmm, dynamic tension?"

"Jeez, Lillian," he muttered. "Where do you get your ideas—from Ernie?"

"Actually, Max, I do find Ernie rather . . . inspirational."

"Serves him right," Max mumbled.

"I beg your pardon?"

"Never mind." He wasn't sure he wanted to know Lillian's plans for Ernie. He was already, as it was, speared on the horns of a moral dilemma. He could either defend his wife's business ethics the way Grace would, if she knew what was going on; or keep her look-alike unclothed body out of the hands of Max's nemesis, Tedsy, who already had enough ideas to tempt Max into reprisals that would definitely put a dent in Grace's business.

He slid a little farther down the slippery slope. The distant voice of his conscience was murmuring that foiling Edmund and deceiving Grace was probably not the way to marital harmony, but it was being drowned out by the more compelling urges of expediency. And anyway, aiding and abetting Lillian's scheme was bound to be better for business than drowning Tedsy in the hot tub, wasn't it?

"Could I have that tube of paint?" Lillian asked, her timing, as usual, lethally accurate.

Max examined his moral dilemma, closed his ears to the voice of conscience, and handed her the tube. "Go to it, Lillian."

Max wasn't in the kitchen consuming milk and cookies, nor was he in the downstairs bar, breaking into Lillian's rum. He was also not on the front porch, or sitting in the dark living room. Stymied, Grace stood in the dark kitchen and polished off a half dozen Oreos and a glass of milk. The idea that suddenly struck her made her go stock-still, jaws frozen in midbite, milk glass poised six inches above the counter.

He was out on the back deck in the hot tub.

Where else would Max Hogan be, sensualist that he was, on a sleepless night in mid-June, but under New England's starry skies in Martin's hot tub? She could picture the scene as if she'd been watching from the doorway: Max, shirtless, his hair tousled, his jeans zipped but not snapped, tugged low on his lean hips from the pressure of his hands in the pockets. He'd probably stood at the door, staring out at the night, then unlatched the screen door and strolled toward the deck, pausing for a moment to gaze up at the sky. Then he would have unzipped his jeans, slid them off, and dropped them on the grass just before gliding, naked, into the hot water.

Grace's milk glass plinked on the counter. She dropped the rest of her cookies into the box, and turned her head toward the deck as sudden heat coursed through her body.

Max, naked in a hot tub, relaxed, sensually aware, his powerful arms stretched out along the edge of the pool, his head thrown back.

She had the screen door half open before she caught herself, glancing down at her hand on the latch as if someone else had put it there. What was she doing, heading outside to gape at Max in a hot tub? She'd already seen him in a hot tub, and she'd thrown him out of her life as a result.

But he'd come back into it, she thought, raising her eyes to the screen. Come back into it and disrupted all her plans, melted all her solid resolutions. And stirred up her longings.

She pushed the door open the rest of the way.

The night was soft, warm for June, but with a whisper of wind that billowed under her sleeveless cotton pajamas and raised goose bumps on her skin. The hot tub, around the corner of the deck, was uncovered, steam rising into the starlit night.

No one, however, was in it.

Grace frowned, stepping closer. She'd been so sure she'd find Max there that she felt annoyed and gave an involuntary, exasperated sigh.

"Oh, for Pete's sake, Grace," she said aloud. "You can't be stood up by a mere expectation."

Of a mere ex-husband.

But *mere* wasn't the word Max brought to mind, and

it didn't very accurately describe the expectation, either.

She crossed her arms in front of her chest, sighed again, and ran her tongue over her teeth, seeking out the last crumbs of chocolate cookie.

They weren't much of a substitute for what she really wanted.

"Grace?"

Her heart leaped and her pulse jumped through a flaming hoop before she registered that it wasn't Max behind her on the deck.

"Oh," she said, turning around. "Edmund."

He frowned, stopping a few feet from her. "Is everything all right?"

"All right? Yes, of course."

"You sounded . . . ah, troubled, when you said my name."

What she'd sounded was disappointed, but it probably wasn't diplomatic to say so. "No, no," she murmured vaguely. She tipped her head back to the sky the way she'd imagined Max doing. The wind whispered promises which, it seemed, were not going to be followed through on. She clasped her palms around her elbows as another gust of wind rippled through her pajamas.

"It's a little cool," Edmund said, adjusting the belt of his silk robe, as if he were considering offering it to her.

Grace guessed her own robeless attire didn't meet the Goodbody standards of either propriety or the

weather, but she didn't want Edmund Goodbody's
robe. She wanted Max's arms or nothing.

"Oh, no," she said again. "It's a nice night." She
strolled closer to the hot tub, gazing into the water.
There was still nobody in it.

"Are you sure everything's all right, Grace? You're
not having any . . . ah, problems?"

"You mean with the appraisal? No. There's nothing
for you to worry about, Edmund. The estate will be
properly auctioned."

"I didn't mean appraisal problems, Grace. I have
the utmost trust in your professional ability."

"Oh. Yes. Thank you," she said, feeling chagrined.
She must have sounded sharper than she'd intended. It
wasn't Edmund's fault that he wasn't Max.

"I was just wondering who uncovered the hot tub,"
she said more brightly, filling in the awkward pause in
the conversation.

"Our handyman, would be my guess," Edmund
said. "The ineffable Max."

"Ineffable?"

"Yes." Edmund smiled at her. "He's turned out to
be surprisingly . . . handy, hasn't he?"

"He has?"

"Well—" Edmund shrugged in a charming, self-
deprecating gesture. "For someone whose primary talents aren't domestic."

"What makes you say that?" Grace asked.

"Oh, I just meant—Max and Lillian. One assumes
she didn't pick him for his facility with a hammer." He
glanced toward her, flicking his hair out of his face, and

smiled again, warily. "Er . . . sorry. No insult meant to your aunt Lillian."

"No, never mind." She looked at him, feeling insulted. "She usually picks them for their income levels, Edmund. No insult meant to your uncle Martin."

"No, of course not. I mean, that's very prudent," Edmund said earnestly. "Really."

"Prudent?"

He flicked his hair out of his face again, his expression anxious. "You don't approve of . . . prudence?"

She took in a breath and uncrossed her arms, swinging them free, then slapping the sides of her legs with her open palms. "No, I guess not, in general. But sometimes . . . I mean, how *do* you pick a spouse?"

Edmund tipped his head to one side. "Chemistry?" he said mischievously.

"Yes," she said, ignoring the mischievous grin. "But can you trust it?"

"I'm not sure I know. If it's strong enough, one doesn't have much choice, does one?"

"No," Grace said. "One doesn't."

Edmund reknotted the tie to his robe, perusing her face, smiling a faint, hard-to-interpret smile. "You know, it is a lovely night, as you mentioned."

"Oh. It is." She crossed her arms again, staring across the hot tub toward the lilac hedge at the far side of the yard. It *was* a lovely night. And where was Max, dammit, when her chemistry was primed, ready to go, and calling out to him?

"My uncle," Edmund offered, after a moment's silence, "was quite a man-about-town in his day."

"Oh, Edmund." She sighed. "I hope he got a good run for his money."

"We have every reason to think he did. And you know, that's all we have, in the final analysis. Live for the moment, that sort of thing."

"Is it?"

"I think so."

Grace moved another step closer to the deserted hot tub and hooked her toes over the edge of it. "But love, Edmund, it's so insubstantial. How can you trust it?"

Edmund strolled casually toward her and curled his own toes over the edge of the tub. "What's the alternative?" he suggested archly.

"Prudence?"

"Yes. Exactly."

He said the words as if they represented deep insight. Grace frowned at him, wondering if he thought he'd answered any of her more serious questions.

"Were you thinking of taking a dip?" he inquired.

"In the hot tub?" she asked. "Oh, no, I couldn't. I . . . just ate." She wasn't about to tell him hot-tubbing was out because she was pregnant. "I had one of those middle-of-the-night cravings for chocolate."

"Oh," he said, sounding disappointed and looking woebegone enough to stir her guilty streak. She knew all about regret for saying the wrong thing, or not saying the right thing.

"Actually," she said, "I was thinking of putting my feet in, but nothing more than that."

"Ah. Feet. What a good idea."

They both sat at the edge of the hot spa, hiked up their pajama legs, and stuck their feet into the warm, swirling water. Silence held sway for a minute or two, punctuated by soft breezes and bubbling water.

"You know, Edmund," Grace murmured, staring down at the distorted slashes of light that represented her feet, "you're much easier to talk to than I thought you were."

"I try my best to please, Grace."

"It seems like, so often, when two people are in love, there's no way to communicate. It's so hard to talk."

"Er . . . is it?"

"It must be all that chemistry. You can't keep it in check, you know? Every look, every touch, it just . . . escalates."

"It does?"

"You know, Edmund, you're the first person I've talked to about this kind of thing in months."

"Am I?"

She sighed. "Except for Lillian. And she just tells me to go for the chemistry."

"Maybe you should," Edmund said.

"Do you think so?"

"Oh, I think so."

The words were fervent.

Grace blinked, slanted Edmund a quick sideways glance, and considered what he meant by that. He was studying her with an expression that was far too meaningful for any meaning she had meant.

Had she been so caught up in her musings about

Max that she'd missed something here? Frowning into the hot tub, she waggled her toes in a nervous reaction.

Edmund waggled his toes too.

Grace stared at him in alarm. He was, she thought with a sinking feeling, staring back.

"Edmund . . . ah . . ."

"Grace."

He leaned toward her, slipped his arm around her shoulders, and moved in toward ground zero, which, she realized belatedly, was her lips.

The screen door to the kitchen slammed open against the outside wall, and someone inside emitted a bellow that expressed pure outrage, absolute intolerance, and no restraint whatsoever.

Edmund clutched her shoulder in panic and craned his head around toward the kitchen.

"Max?" Grace said.

"You got that right, babe." He charged toward her across the deck.

Grace pulled her feet out of the water and scrambled to stand up. "Where have you been?" she demanded. "Hiding in the kitchen? All this time?"

"Long enough to see what's going on here."

"What *is* going on here?" Edmund put in, sounding feeble compared to Max.

"Nothing is going on here!" Grace declared.

"Oh yeah?" Max retorted. "You call this *nothing*?"

"You call this *restraint*?"

"Compared to the way you're carrying on out here?" He huffed indignantly, ripped his hand through his hair, then shoved it into his pocket as if he didn't trust himself not to do something even less restrained than shouting. "Glomming chocolate cookies in the kitchen with lover-boy here? Traipsing around in your pajamas, throwing your head back to the stars? Necking beside the hot tub?"

"I resent those implications! They're entirely unjustified!"

"You want *justified*? Well, let me tell you this: If you think you're making another move toward that hot tub, all bets are off, babe!"

Grace glared at him, too incensed to speak. After a short pause Edmund asked, "What, exactly, are we betting on?"

Grace shot him a distracted glance, and Max gave him a level glare that incorporated a couple of fantasies about drownings.

"I can't believe you're standing here, Max Hogan, telling *me* not to get into a hot tub."

"I can't believe you're bringing that up again."

"Why not? You think you had any more right than I do to get into a hot tub? Says who?"

"Says *Baby and Child Care*," he shot back. "*I'm* not pregnant!"

"What?" Edmund said, sounding confused.

"Let me tell you something, Max Hogan," Grace spat, pinning him with one finger in the center of his chest. "I've read *Baby and Child Care* too. And according to the chapter on parenting, *we* are the pregnant couple!"

"Oh my God," Edmund said, staring at Grace. "You've been having an affair with Lillian's boyfriend?"

"Of course not!" Grace told him, exasperated. "Max is my husband."

Edmund blinked. "Lillian's been having an affair with your husband?"

Both of them turned toward him, their argument silenced momentarily.

"Good God," Edmund muttered. "What kind of a family is this? I mean, who is getting into the hot tub with whom?"

"Tedsy," Max said. "*You* are getting into the hot tub. Solo."

He gave Edmund a firm push with one arm and watched him stagger backward, then drop into the sunken tub with a spectacular splash.

"Edmund!" Grace cried.

Max took her by the arm, turning her away from the scene of Edmund floundering in hot water, and hustled her into the kitchen.

"Max!" she protested breathlessly.

He whirled her around to face him, pulled her flush against his bare chest, and brought his mouth down onto hers.

His hand clasped the back of her head and tilted her face to give him full access to her mouth. Grace made a sound that started as a protest, an automatic reaction to the outrageous arrogance he'd just demonstrated, but ended up as a soft, sexy reaction to the soft, sexy arrogance he was demonstrating right now.

His tongue flicked along the edge of her lip. She opened her mouth to accept it and let her own hands roam around his waist to the hollow of his spine until their bodies fit together with well-remembered, sensual practice, hip-to-hip, mouth-to-mouth. A wave of dizzy, giddy sensation wavered over her like flickering electricity.

The screen door creaked open, but neither Max nor Grace paid any attention as Edmund came through it. He paused, holding the door, witnessing the ardent proceedings of the couple that obviously didn't know he existed, then squelched by on wet feet, with no comment.

Grace moaned as Max's hands slipped inside the back of her pajamas.

"Gracie?" he said, the word slurred against her mouth. "D'zis mean you wanna ac' like a preggant coupow?"

"Oh, Max," she answered. "I thought you'd never ask."

He bent from the waist, scooped her up, and carried her up the stairs.

TEN

At the top of the stairs, Max paused at the open door of Grace's room and leaned a shoulder against the door-jamb, panting. Grace wiggled, trying to get down.

"What are you doing?" He clutched her more tightly.

"Put me down, Max. You'll get a hernia."

"Worth it." He staggered into the room and put her down on the rumpled bed, then leaned over her, pushing her gently back to the pillows, and covered her mouth with his.

Between Max's panting and Grace's muffled sound of surprise, it was a breathless kiss, but what it lacked in finesse it made up for in passion. Max's fingers speared into her hair, his mouth moved provocatively on hers, and he made a sound deep in his throat that was pure, raw desire.

She was nearly as breathless as he when she cupped

his face with her hands, holding him away from her. "Max!"

He lifted his head reluctantly.

"You left the door open."

"That's all right, Gracie," he murmured, moving in again, "Tedsy's in the other wing."

"But—there could be somebody else up, Max."

That stopped him. He gazed at her, and a flicker of intelligence came into his eyes, though it was all but overwhelmed by passion. "You mean . . . like Lillian?"

"Yes. Or—"

"Lillian," he mumbled, pushing himself up. "Right. Don't move, Grace." He bolted from the bed, jogged across the room, and shut the door. As an afterthought, he got a straight chair and propped it backward under the doorknob, then turned and eyed the dresser.

"Max? What are you doing?"

"Keeping Lillian out." He was grinning slightly, but Grace wasn't sure he was kidding.

She propped herself higher on the bed, but didn't, on second thought, voice an objection to Max's extremes. Lillian did seem to have a way of intruding on their intimate moments.

"Gracie? You're not going anywhere, are you?"

She met his gaze, and her breath caught. His eyes, in the soft light from the bedside lamp, had become a dark, feral blue. The tension in his jaw emphasized the harsh, masculine planes of his face, and a shiver inched its way up her spine. She felt a sweet longing in all the hollows of her body, from the soles of her feet to the dip above her collarbones. She wanted Max's mouth there, in all those places, warm and sensual and knowing.

She wanted to make love with Max Hogan, who knew her better than anyone else ever had, whom she knew better than she had ever known anyone else. She wanted the man she'd given herself to, body and soul, to claim her again, to reestablish the knowledge, to reaffirm what they both knew.

"Max," she said, her voice husky. "Come here."

His eyes brightened with a ferocious intent that struck her as beautiful. The whole man, she thought, was beautiful: the tension in his jaw, the square muscles of his chest that rippled when he slid his thumbs into the pockets of his jeans, as if to keep himself from hauling her into his arms. He moved toward her with careful restraint, and he wasn't a man of natural restraint, she thought. He was a man of impulse, of reckless animal passion, of beautiful, barbarian instincts.

Her own barbarian instincts swirled through her, hot and sweet and highly uncivilized. Before Max had even settled himself on the bed next to her, she was reaching for him, pulling him toward her for a kiss she couldn't, suddenly, go without any longer.

He clutched her upper arms and lifted her to him, giving her more than her measure of passion for passion. "Ah, Gracie," he murmured, "you are so . . . so . . . Whatever you want, Grace, I'll do it. Whatever way you want me—"

"I want chemistry, Max," she breathed, letting her

head fall back as he pressed his mouth to her throat. "Pure chemistry. I want to forget everything else."

"You got it, babe. All of it. Chemistry, physics, biology . . . hell, Latin, if you want it."

She did. She wanted all of it. She wanted all the reckless, abandoned acts she'd ever imagined doing with a man. She wanted all the reckless, abandoned acts she'd ever imagined her aunt Lillian doing with a man. She wanted Max Hogan with his jeans off.

She slipped her hand around the snap above the zipper, and heard the sharp intake of his breath as he sucked in his stomach. She tugged the snap free and pulled on the zipper tab. There was nothing underneath the zipper but the essential Max.

Grace expelled a long breath as she let go of the zipper and curled her hand around him. It was like touching tensile, silk-shrouded danger. He let out an agonized, barbarian groan that thrilled her to the soul. He was hot, he was wild, and he was hers, transfixed by her touch. She stroked him, and a quiver like Lucifer's ecstasy rippled through him. His hands tightened convulsively on her arms, and the sound from his throat was strangled, too much pleasure to express.

She felt a surge of uncivilized feminine power as heady and unstoppable as the Charge of the Light Brigade. She *couldn't* have stopped herself. Two months of denial had been merely the storing up of the undeniable animal impulses Max had released in her the day they met.

He caught her wrist and dragged her hand away from him, muttering something she couldn't understand while he pulled her against him. He kissed her with ferocious, raw intensity, then set her back on the pillows and unfastened the buttons on the front of her pajamas. He didn't stop when he'd released the last one. He hooked his fingers into the elastic waist of her pajama bottoms and yanked them down over her hips and along her thighs. She pulled one foot free and kicked the pajamas across the room, oblivious to the fact that they landed half in and half out of Lucifer's aquarium.

Max uttered a word she recognized as an uncivilized profanity, but he said it with the kind of reverence and wonderment she associated with church.

For no reason she could justify, she paused for a second, touched his face, and murmured, "For better or for worse, Max."

His mouth curved in a swift, volatile smile. "For as long as we're both alive, Gracie."

"I think we are," she murmured.

"Oh, yeah, babe."

They were. Max knew it in every brain cell, every sensitized nerve. They were definitely alive. He was definitely, positively, ravenously conscious. They were both alive. Maybe . . . all three of them, he thought with a jolt of insight that rocked him to the base of his brain. They were not only alive, they were part of the life chain. They were reproducing. They were making a baby. He felt a surging electrical bolt of sensuality that would have paralyzed him except that his hand was already moving toward Gracie, toward the still flat curve of her stomach, the sweet, powerful, feminine geography of her hips, the graceful apex of her thighs, adorned by a thatch of dark curls.

"Is this what you want, Gracie?" he asked, stroking her.

She hesitated, catching her breath, then whispered, "Yes."

"And this?"

"Oh, Max." She clutched his shoulders. "Oh, Max, I've waited for this."

"You have?"

"Yes. I came looking for you," she confessed, sighing. "I couldn't imagine where you were."

"You came looking for me?"

She opened her eyes, searching his. "Yes."

"Just . . . now?"

"Where were you?" she murmured, caressing the back of his neck with her fingers.

Max's conscience made a strident, but feeble shriek that, if he'd been listening, would have sounded like, *In the attic*. Some shred of common sense, however, not to mention sexual interest, deleted the accompanying phrase: *with Lillian*.

What could that possibly have to do with him and Grace, making love, making magic, making a baby? They were ordained, they were electric. They were a pregnant couple.

Something a lot like his conscience told him that blurting out Grace's secret, dumping her current client in a hot tub, and making deals with Lillian were not necessarily the behavior of one half of a pregnant couple, but Max was too beguiled to care, too enthralled by his wife's sweet, long-needed sensuality to decipher the nuances of his conscience.

Grace wanted him. He wanted Grace. When he sank himself into her, nothing else in God's far-spread earth mattered.

Grace Hogan was his wife, the mother of his child, the love of his life.

If he blew a few fuses, he'd fix them later.

Afterward, the world drifted slowly back to Grace's consciousness. Her cheek was against Max's shoulder, his arm holding her, his profile backlit by the glow of the bedside lamp. His eyes were closed, his hair tousled, and he was sprawled crosswise on the bed, but he managed to look smug nonetheless.

"Max?" she murmured.

"Mm?" He turned his head, caressing her temple with his cheek.

"You look smug."

"Yeah." He opened his eyes and looked at her. "That's what happens when you make those noises."

"You mean when I . . . ah, sigh?"

His mouth curved into a smug grin. "Yeah. When you . . . sigh."

She smiled, feeling smug herself, fulfilled and satisfied. "We should have done this long ago, Max."

There was a pause. "We did," he said.

"Well, yes, but—" She didn't finish the sentence, because she wasn't quite sure what she meant. Or that Max would get it, whatever it was.

His hand brushed down the outside of her arm and across her hip and came to rest on her stomach. "Grace," he said momentarily, "I was thinking. . . ."

She was fairly sure of the direction of his thoughts, but he took so long to get specific, she finally said, "What?"

"Maybe we could get an MG minivan. If they make one. You know, for Max and Grace?"

"An *MG minivan*?"

"You don't think the baby would feel left out, do you? Because we could name her something that starts with *M* or *G*. You thought about that?"

"Not in those terms," she said. "What if it's a boy?"

"Well, then, it would have to be a different name, of course."

"Mm."

"Grace?" His hand moved, just slightly, on her stomach. "You think it has little baby thoughts?"

She turned toward him, dislodging his hand from her stomach, and propped herself on one elbow, the better to stare at him and wonder where he got these ideas. "About what?" she asked.

He shook his head, a man perplexed. "I don't know."

"Max? Is that what you were thinking about when we were . . . ?"

"Well, no. Not exactly." He put his hand back on her hip, proprietarily. "I wasn't thinking about the baby then. I mean, I didn't *forget* about the baby, you know? At least not—"

"Max?"

"What?"

"It's all right."

"You weren't thinking about the baby, either?"

She shook her head.

"No. I didn't think so." The smug expression was back on his face. Grace felt a small ripple of sexuality at the sight of him.

"Gracie? Do you think the baby . . . ah, liked it?"

"Liked it?"

"Yeah, you know—when its parents made love."

Max's smile had gotten a bit more smug. She had a feeling she knew where this was going too. "I don't know, Max. It's pretty small. Floating around in its little pool."

Max's hand convulsed for a moment on her hip. He looked alarmed. "You mean, like Lucifer? With his spasms?"

His hand tightened. The alarm in his expression was rapidly being aggravated by worry, panic, and—yes, Grace decided—guilt.

Good heavens. Tell a man he was one half of a pregnant couple and he immediately started feeling irrational guilt? What did that mean? Hormones?

Was he going to start practicing restraint?

"Max," she said, laying her hand on his chest, "I don't think it's anything like Lucifer."

"You don't?" His eyes darkened, and she saw a flare of something unrestrained and beautiful in the depths of his gaze. It was something she wanted to encourage, Grace decided.

"No, I don't," she said, moving her hand in a slow circle. "And anyway, Lucifer liked it."

Max didn't offer any more irrational guilt.

Or any more restraint, either.

Max woke to the sound of someone knocking on the door, waking him from a wonderful dream in which he'd been holding Grace and . . .

And he *was* holding Grace, he realized, amazed and awestruck for an instant as the details of the night before scrolled through his mind.

A self-satisfied smile crept up the corners of his mouth. Of course he was holding Grace. He'd won her back, triumphed over circumstance and rivals, received the rewards of a noble heart and true masculine courage, not to mention charm and a certain gift for . . . consorting.

His arm tightened, and Max's smugness slipped into something more sensual as Grace turned her face toward his and murmured a warm and sleepy syllable. "Grace," he whispered into her tousled hair.

More frantic knocking interrupted his half-formed intentions. Max frowned toward the door.

"Grace?" a voice hissed from the other side of it. "Grace? Are you awake?"

A masculine voice. A *familiar* masculine voice. A familiar masculine voice that Max had vanquished in noble combat. What was Tedsy doing outside the door at a time like this, trying to wake up Max's wife?

Max eased his arm out from under Grace's shoulder, rolled out of bed, and stomped across the floor to the door.

"Grace?"

"What do you want?" Max whispered back.

"There's . . . ah, something going on downstairs," Edmund said. "Everyone else seems to be up."

"So?"

"My mother has started bringing out items from the back room. Eloise, as a result, felt compelled to bring down a few items from the attic. And Lillian has . . . ah, entered the picture."

Entered the picture? Did that mean she'd entered *the picture?*

"They're all arguing," Edmund added unhappily.

Good, Max thought. Why didn't Edmund go back and join the fracas, and he and Grace could get on with . . .

"Max?" Grace said in a sleepy voice. "Who are you talking to?"

"Talking?" Max said, giving her an innocuous grin.

"Oh, no," Edmund continued through the door. "It's nothing as civilized as *talking*. I think there may be violence any moment now."

"No way," Max said.

"Oh, yes. There's going to be some property damaged."

"Max? What's going on?"

"Nothing important," Max muttered.

"Nothing important?" Edmund exclaimed. "These are priceless antiques! We need an appraiser!"

"You need a referee!" Max told him.

"Exactly! What do think I've been trying to say?"

Max glared at the door, ready with several replies, although he wasn't sure he should waste them on some bozo who still, apparently, thought he was talking to Grace.

"All right, Edmund," Grace called from across the room, bailing out his rival with what Max thought was entirely too forgiving a spirit. "I'll be right down."

"The sooner the better," Edmund said.

Speak for yourself, buddy, Max thought, but it was too late to express the sentiment. Grace was already hustling out of bed, her pajamas gathered in front of her, obscuring all the charms Max would have liked to explore further. With acute disappointment he watched her cross the room to the closet and pull out a pair of pants and a shirt, which she tossed onto the rumpled bed. Still holding the pajamas against her, she rummaged in the top bureau drawer for underwear.

She glanced toward him, her eyes soft and vulnerable and sexy, her white lacy undies clutched in one hand. "Max? Don't just stand there! Go down and mediate for a couple of minutes, would you? While I take a shower? Just keep them from destroying anything?"

He sighed, nodded, and with a sense of opportunity lost, shuffled across the room and picked up his jeans.

Hostilities were in full swing when he got down to the living room, and Edmund was in the midst of the fray, planted between Lillian and his mother, directly in front of a white-draped easel from which Marian was trying to snatch off the covering while Lillian tried to prevent her. Lillian was winning because Marian's attention was partly diverted to Eloise, who was scurrying back and forth moving a bunch of glass lamps out of harm's way.

"*Where* did you get that Tiffany?" Marian demanded, temporarily letting go of the white sheet. Lillian moved in to get both hands around the frame, holding the drapery in place.

"From the attic." Eloise set the lamp on an end table and added helpfully, "There are about five dozen of them up there."

"Five *dozen*?"

Lillian lifted painting and easel together and staggered back a step.

"Lillian!" Edmund pleaded, extending his arms toward the painting but leery of touching it. "What are you doing? You're going to drop it!"

"Don't drop it yet!" Eloise scurried around behind Lillian to rescue another lamp.

Marian lunged and came up with a handful of sheet.

"Mother! Please!"

"Let go!" Lillian yanked at the painting. "This artwork isn't being unveiled until Grace is here to catalog it!"

"We'll see about that!" Marian snatched at more sheet.

Lillian tightened her hold.

Max made tracks toward the fracas, which clearly was beyond Tedsy's capacity. He reached Lillian just as a corner of the frame poked through its concealing drapery. Marian made a grab for the torn fabric, and

Lillian sprawled backward with the painting and thumped against Max's chest.

He got his hands on the frame and lifted it over Lillian's head, trailing the sheet across her face.

She slapped the material out of her way and turned toward him. "Put that down, Max! Grace hasn't cataloged it yet!"

"Good," he said. "Why don't I put it back up in the attic where Grace can catalog it later? Next week, maybe."

"It can't wait until next week. It's going to be the first item in the auction!"

"And *who*, I'd like to know, made *that* decision?" Marian demanded.

"*Grace* will make that decision," Lillian said, "when she sees it. It's the perfect item to warm up a crowd."

"No doubt about that," Eloise grumbled. "Look what it's done for this one."

"What did you do with Grace, anyway?" Lillian asked, a little peeved that Max was still holding the painting out of her reach.

Marian rounded on Lillian. "Are you speaking to my son? Are you implying that Edmund and Grace have been doing anything improper?"

"No, but if it gives you a thrill to imagine the deed, don't let me stop you, Marian."

Max, outraged by the idea of Edmund and Grace, let the painting dip a few inches.

"Mother, I'm not—"

"Damn right you're not!" Max shouted.

Marian saw her advantage and took it. She darted

in, nabbed a corner of the sheet, and whipped it off the painting.

Stunned silence greeted the revelation. Not even a Tiffany lamp shade stirred.

"Oh my God," Marian breathed. "It's a satanic altar."

"Altered, all right," Eloise muttered.

"Is it . . . a woman?" Edmund inquired.

"Is it even dry?" Max asked.

"*Someone,*" Grace said from the bottom of the stairs, "has got to be kidding."

Max peered around the painting to meet her gaze, his expression wary, desperate . . . and *guilty*, Grace realized with a shock. She'd had enough experience with guilt to know it when she saw it.

And she was seeing it now.

"Gracie . . ." he said. His voice held a trace of apology that might as well have been a full confession.

She descended the last step and narrowed her eyes on the painting, held aloft in Max's arms, as she came closer.

He let his arms sag, watching her face. "Gracie. Don't look like that, sweetheart."

Grace felt her jaw tighten. She touched an index finger to the surface of the painting. A few dots of paint came away on her fingertip. She pinned Aunt Lillian with a level glare and unlocked her jaw enough to ask, "Watercolor? Over oils?"

"Well, I didn't, of course, want anything *permanent,*" Lillian murmured.

"Of course you wouldn't," Grace snapped, her temper surging. "I've known that, ever since you threw away all my childhood treasures to redecorate my room!"

"Your childhood treasures?" Lillian repeated. "You mean that night-light?"

"I mean, your *modus operandi*, Aunt Lillian. Paint over anything that doesn't suit your notions!"

"Oh, jeez, Grace," Max said, sounding stricken. "I didn't think of that."

Grace ripped a corner off the torn sheet and rubbed carefully at the painted figure's face. The black paint came off onto the rag, and Lillian's immortalized features appeared under the makeshift veil.

"Grace?" Edmund said, moving in closer. "Is that you?"

"You've actually painted over it?" Marian breathed, turning toward Lillian.

Eloise poked Marian in the ribs. "And don't you wish you'd thought of it, Marian?"

Edmund rubbed his thumb over the figure's shoulder, dislodging a little more paint.

"Back off, Edmund!" Max warned.

At Max's outburst, Grace rounded on him, her anger at being duped sharply refocused on him. "And you knew about this, didn't you, Max?"

He sighed.

"Well, I didn't, Max. I didn't have a clue. I thought you were figuring out lawn mowers and fuses, proving yourself as a handyman. I didn't know you were scheming with—with my *aunt*, to do—I don't know what!"

"She wanted to buy the painting, Grace. She

thought it should have been hers when she divorced Martin, and last night when I—"

"*Last night?*"

Max made a faint, inarticulate sound and reached toward her.

Grace brushed him off and stepped back. "Last night? When, last night? Before or after we had our . . . tryst for the weekend?"

"Max and *Grace?*" Marian said querulously. "What on earth is going on here?"

Max stared at Grace in shocked silence, then said, disbelieving, "That wasn't any tryst for the weekend, Gracie."

She crossed her arms in front of her. "Before or after?"

"Before or . . . What difference does it make?"

"Before or after we talked about babies' names, and whether we . . . would forget about it, and whether it knew we were . . ." Her voice trailed off, and she swiped at her cheeks and glared at him.

Max gazed back at her, his mouth wrinkled into a worried line. He pushed his hands into his pockets and said, "Before, all right?"

She stared at him, feeling as if she'd been kicked.

"Before *what?*" Marian whined.

"Mother," Edmund said, sounding desperate, "please. Why don't we all go into the kitchen and get a cup of coffee?"

No one moved.

"Gracie . . . I was going to tell you. I mean, I know I should have, but—"

"Before," she repeated. She'd meant the word to be scathing, but she couldn't keep the tremble out of her voice, and, to her disgust, her eyes filled with tears.

Max reached for her again, but she backed away.

"Sweetheart," he said. "Come on. You never had anything you meant to tell me, and didn't?"

A flush of heat flared in her cheeks. She pressed a hand to her stomach, her fingers curling unconsciously into a fist.

Oh, yes, she'd had something she'd meant to tell him and didn't. Her pregnancy. She drew in a shaky breath, but she couldn't get all the air she needed into her suddenly constricted lungs. The familiar knot of panic in her stomach expanded into her chest.

Eloise was appraising her as if she thought Grace had been awfully late arriving at her conclusions. Lillian was glancing from Max to Grace with a little frown of puzzlement on her face, no doubt analyzing the possibilities in this new situation. Edmund was staring unhappily at his feet as if he wished they'd take him elsewhere.

What kind of a family is this? Edmund's comment of the night before echoed through Grace's mind, with a painful variation. What kind of a mother was she going to be, when she couldn't even manage an estate appraisal without being scammed by one of Lillian's transparent schemes, aided and abetted by her own husband?

Although she doubted that Lillian had really needed anyone's help. Grace had practically duped herself on her own, throwing herself into Max's arms, abandoning herself to mindless passion, telling him she just wanted chemistry.

At least Max had been honest about that part, she thought, castigating herself with every new, guilty insight. At least he'd admitted all he wanted was to get back into her bed, any way he could manage it. No doubt it hadn't been convenient to tell her about Lillian's paint job before they'd made love.

"I just thought," Max said, giving her a tentative but hopeful smile, pulling his hands out of his pockets, "maybe you could understand, you know?"

"What?" she said tightly. "Your not telling me about Lillian? That makes us even?"

"Well." He shrugged, as if that took care of the problem, and why make it any more difficult. "That's one way to look at it."

Another surge of anger shot through her, and Grace latched on to it, nursed it, let it flare unchecked because it was easier to feel furious than to sort through the agonizing tangle of emotions churning in her gut, because she'd lived for two months with self-doubt she couldn't acknowledge, because it was safer to lash out at Max than to give in to her fears.

"No," she gritted. "That doesn't make us even. I think you should leave, Max."

"Leave?" He frowned at her. "What? Leave here?"

"Never mind. I'll leave."

"Gracie, what are you—?"

She turned on her heel and hurried across the living room. Max trailed after her, and she confronted him at the bottom of the stairs. "Just leave me alone, Max! Just stay out of my way!"

Max watched from the bottom landing, dumbfounded, as she sprinted up half the flight of stairs, then he cursed under his breath and sprinted after her.

"Gracie—"

She dashed into her room and slammed the door.

Max opened it. She was pulling her suitcase out from under the bed. "You can't mean this," he said. "Over Lillian's paint job?"

She flung the suitcase on the bed and yanked open a drawer.

"Grace, you're working here. You're the appraiser."

"*Was* the appraiser. You took care of that for me, Max Hogan. You and Aunt Lillian."

"Oh, come on. You can't believe that Tedsy's going to fire you. I mean, just because Lillian painted over a picture of herself." He paused. "And I did push him into the hot tub, but that was—"

"I don't know what he's going to do!" She ripped out the last of her clothes and stuffed them into the suitcase. "It doesn't matter, anyway."

"It doesn't?"

"I'm not leaving because of Tedsy, Max," she raged at him. "I'm leaving because of you!" She wrestled the suitcase off the bed and stepped around Max toward the door.

He watched her take a couple more steps, then moved again, grabbing her suitcase.

"Let go!"

"At least let me carry it for you."

She relinquished it with a wordless, angry look, then stomped out of the room and down the stairs.

Outside the house, standing beside Grace's car, Max hesitated again, jiggling the suitcase in one hand, studying Grace as she stood with her back to him, arms crossed, body language stubborn, angry, and withdrawn.

"Grace," he said finally. "I'm sorry."

Grace glanced at him. "Good," she bit out, hurting him, feeling spiteful and small but still too afraid to let go of her anger.

He flinched, swallowed hard, then dropped the suitcase on the sidewalk and covered his face with one hand. After a moment he sighed and looked at her. "I didn't think it was that big a deal," he said. "I didn't . . . oh, hell. I just didn't think at all. I only wanted us to get back together, Gracie. I wanted . . ."

"Well," she said, "we're not." She pulled open the door to her car and got in.

Max took a step toward her and crouched down on one knee, one arm on the door, preventing her from closing it. Instead she rummaged in her handbag for her car keys, avoiding his eyes.

"Grace?"

Her keys didn't seem to be there. She dug into the bag, increasingly desperate, then finally looked up at him and snapped, "What?"

At her tone Max dropped his head and pinched the bridge of his nose, his shoulders slumped, his free hand dangling as he rested his wrist on his knee.

Her fingers closed around the car keys, and she

pulled them out of her bag, then clutched them against the steering wheel, her knuckles white.

"I was wrong, Max," she said, her gaze glued to the windshield straight ahead. "I should have told you. All right. I apologize. Is that what you want?"

He didn't move, even when she finally glanced toward him. At last he shook his head and gestured helplessly with one hand. "No. That's not what I want. I don't want you to be sorry. You know what I want." His voice was low, quiet, persuasive. "I showed you what I want last night. And you showed me. And we were—"

"Stop it! Stop it, Max! We were lying to each other! I was desperate not to actually have to *talk* to you, and you were scheming behind my back with Lillian!" She turned away, disgusted. "She must have been so *pleased* that we'd gotten together. It suited her plan so well."

Max stared at her again, nonplussed by her bitterness, searching for a key to it, trying to puzzle his way through to her. "Come on, sweetheart," he said. "Lillian was just trying to help, in her own way. You know that. She's been like a parent to you. She'd always be there if you really needed her."

"That's your idea of what a parent should be? Well, I'll tell you something, Max: That's exactly what I thought your idea was. And you haven't shown me anything to change my mind!"

Stunned, he let his hand drop from the door of the car, then he grabbed again for the armrest, as if he needed it to hold himself up. "*That's* what this is about?"

Grace shot him a look, but didn't speak.

"It *is*, isn't it?" He blew out a breath, incredulous, then stared at Grace's face as a flush of guilty color gave away her answer.

"That is it," he said. "It doesn't have a damn thing to do with that painting, does it? You don't think I'm responsible enough to meet your standards for being a parent, do you? You think I'm going to turn out like your own parents and want to dump the kid off on Lillian. Or maybe you think we're both going to turn out like that, huh? We're both going to be lousy parents."

She fumbled her key into the ignition, her hands shaking badly.

"Gracie—look at me, dammit."

"Let go of my door, Max!"

He ignored her demand. "What do you want, Gracie? Some perfect, TV-sitcom kind of family man, who can change a fuse in five seconds and mow a lawn in fifteen?"

She shook her head.

"Because let me tell you something. Maybe there's more to being a parent than that."

"How would you know?" she flung out, hurting him, hurting herself.

"Give me a break, Gracie." He reared his head back, assessing her. "You gave me a break last night," he said softly, a final attempt to reach her. "Did you regret that?"

"No!" she shouted, gripping the wheel tightly. "I regretted it this morning!"

A muscle in his cheek ticked, and he didn't make any attempt to hide the raw pain that crossed his face, but he didn't argue further. He rose to his feet slowly, his gaze on her averted face.

He reached for her suitcase, put it in the backseat, and slammed the rear door shut. "Okay," he said, a tight, quiet word as he stepped back to let her close her door. "I guess the next move is yours."

He stood perfectly still and watched her as she drove off, all the way down the street.

ELEVEN

Grace drove across town with her throat closed against tears and her hands wrapped around the steering wheel so tightly, her fingers ached, holding on to her composure only long enough to reach the haven of her rambling, family-sized house. But when she'd let herself in and slumped back against the front door, the futility of her impulsive flight from Martin Goodbody's estate—and Max—washed over her in a wave of despair. What had made her think she could bear to be here with herself once she got home?

Hugging her elbows, Grace shuffled through the front hallway to the kitchen, then stood in the middle of the room, staring around her. She'd have to repaint the cabinets soon. A little more paint had chipped off, revealing the dingy cream color beneath the faded blue, and even that was worn through here and there to the red layer beneath.

A cracked window needed to be reglazed. The leaky

faucet hadn't healed itself. The ceiling could use another coat of plaster, and her table with the wobbly leg had been on her list of projects for a long time.

But, staring at the table, Grace saw not a pleasant two-hour project but a long, lonely afternoon of work. A whole string of long, lonely afternoons. The terrifying prospect of empty weekends stretching out in front of her, and endless miserable nights while she waited for the baby to grow inside her and wondered what it would be like, with no one to share her concerns or her worries.

Or her hopes that maybe she would be a natural as a mother, that maybe she could give this baby as much love and security and joy as any child needed. That maybe she and Max and their baby could be the kind of family she'd longed for in that vulnerable part of her soul that Max had always touched.

The wobbly-legged table grew misty, then blurred in front of her. Grace gulped back a sob, dashed at her eyes with the heel of her hand, and stumbled across the kitchen to the paper towels to blow her nose.

Disconsolately she wandered back to the front hall, staring at the phone, listening to the remorseful voice in her head telling her to call him and apologize. But she'd said such hurtful things.

And some of them . . . some of them . . . She'd been right about some of them, hadn't she?

The phone didn't answer her question. Nor did the empty hall table where Lucifer's aquarium usually sat.

Grace's eyes widened, and she touched her fingers

to her lips, realizing suddenly that she'd left him behind.

She'd gone off and left Lucifer behind.

She sank down on the bottom landing of her hall stairs, leaned her head against the banister, and burst into tears.

By that evening, Grace was convinced she'd cried enough to take the finish off every cabinet and tabletop in the house. Around noon she'd broken down and called Max, but there had been no answer at his apartment or his office, and she couldn't try him at the Goodbody house because the phone there hadn't been connected.

Halfway through the afternoon she decided to drive back to Martin's house, but when she put the key into the ignition, she burst into a new spate of tears. Fifteen minutes later she dragged herself back to the house to splash cold water on her red and swollen eyes.

She made herself eat a sandwich and take the vitamin pill her obstetrician had prescribed, but the sandwich made her stomach hurt—the first smidgen of morning sickness she'd suffered—and the queasiness made her worry about whether crying was good for her baby.

At six o'clock the phone rang.

Grace's heart lurched with a wrenching, ambivalent onslaught of dread, confusion, and crazy, nerve-zinging hope, and she hurried into the front hall to pick it up.

Oh Max. I'm sorry. I didn't mean it.

But it was Lillian's voice, not Max's, that said, "Grace?" For a moment she couldn't speak.

"Grace? Are you there?"

"Yes," Grace said, her voice hoarse. "I'm here, Aunt Lillian."

After a few seconds' silence her aunt asked cautiously, "Is Max there with you?"

Grace felt another fat, misery-laden lump rise into her throat. "No," she said, the word choked and emotional.

Lillian's reply was a four-letter word.

"My thoughts exactly, Aunt Lillian."

"Except that you don't use that kind of language," Lillian said.

"Yes, I do. I just don't like to admit it. I just like to pretend I'm a-above all that. But I'm not. Which just makes me a h-hypocrite, Aunt Lillian." Her throat thickened, and her eyes filled up again. "As well as being self-righteous and t-temperamental and a l-lousy estate appraiser and t-terrible parent."

"Oh, Grace," Lillian said, distressed. "That can't be true. Why, you spotted the watercolor overlay on that painting at first glance."

"I'm s-sorry, Aunt Lillian."

"Oh, you don't have to apologize." Lillian sighed. "It is your job, after all. And you *are* good at it."

"Good at my job? Aunt Lillian, I don't know if I even have a job anymore."

"Well, of course you do. Edmund was very specific about that, although his reasoning was a little specious. He said something to the effect that you were the only appraiser in the state who could be induced to believe the shenanigans of the relatives."

"He did?"

"Yes. He must have been referring to Eloise. Or Marian."

"Must have been," Grace choked out.

"And he's right, of course. Marian had the *effrontery* to call the police," Lillian reported. "But fortunately, it was that good-looking friend of Max's who came over."

"Ernie?"

"He was entirely *reasonable* about the whole affair. Marian was fit to be tied. Eloise, thank God, kept a low profile. She doesn't like . . . er, unsolicited publicity." There was a pause, then Grace heard Lillian's muffled voice saying, "Oh, no, no. Nothing to worry about." At normal volume again, she said, "Ernie says—"

"Ernie? He's with you?"

"Oh, yes. I'm talking on his car phone, actually."

"You're talking on a *police* phone?"

"Yes. Ernie says quote, 'Hit him with the punch bowl if you feel the need, but don't break his heart.' "

Over the blood rushing in her ears Grace heard her own voice saying sadly, "I think I already have, Aunt Lillian."

"Well—but only once or twice, Grace. And that's just part of . . . well, being young and in love."

"I have been *young*," Grace said. "As in adolescent and immature. I've been blaming Max for all my own shortcomings, all my own doubts. He was right, Aunt Lillian. You don't have to be a perfect, TV-sitcom father to make a good parent. I've just been so . . .

s-scared—" She broke off, forced down another sob, and clutched the phone tighter.

There was a momentary pause. "Grace? I never knew you cared so much about that little fairy princess night-light. I think I must still have it somewhere, up in the attic. I could look for it."

"Th-that's okay, Aunt Lillian. It's not really important."

Lillian said, with uncharacteristic gentleness, "Is there anything I can do, Grace?"

Grace drew in a shaky breath, then said, "Yes, Aunt Lillian. There is, now that you mention it. Could you feed Lucifer for me?"

"Lucifer? But he's gone."

"Gone? Where did he go?"

"Max has him. He took him before lunch. That's why I thought he'd gone to your house."

"No." Grace's heart thumped like a twenty-horse-power diesel turning over on a cold start. "He said . . ." She swallowed hard. "He said the next move was mine, Aunt Lillian."

"Well, then, Grace," Lillian said, not unkindly, "you'd better make it."

The Blue Moon was half full of Friday-afternoon celebrants when Grace walked into the restaurant and made her way toward the bar in back. She was a woman on a mission. Max's red Mustang was parked outside at the curb, with neither Max nor her fish sitting in it. One or the other of them had to be in here.

Draft beer and grilled hamburgers scented the air, dim lighting did its best to protect the anonymity of customers, and Dwight Yoakam was crooning a ballad she hadn't heard before, about restless hearts and arrested love.

A blond, ponytailed beer drinker grinned at her from his table when she hesitated just inside the door, then he got up, wove his way through the tables toward her, and offered to buy her a beer.

"I'm looking for someone," Grace told him. "Black leather jacket, dark hair, with a fish."

Her would-be beer buyer eyed her skeptically, muttered, "I guess I don't have the qualifications you want, honey," and retreated without an argument.

She found the man with the right qualifications sitting under the moose with his back to her, a full glass of beer in front of him and Lucifer, in her crystal punch bowl, next to his elbow.

Grace stood still, watching him, feeling her heart start to thump harder as sweet, hot emotions welled up in her chest. How on God's green earth had she managed to live two months without him? How could she possibly have ever faced the idea of spending the rest of her life without Max? Divorcing him, raising their baby without him?

She saw him turn his head slightly toward the fish, murmur a word or two, and lean closer to get a better look.

Grace felt something unfold deep inside her. *Max.* Her sweet, macho, sexy, responsible Max. Everything about him—the way he hunched his muscular shoulders, the way his unruly hair curled over his collar—was right for her, right for them both to grow up together, to face their fears and hopes together, to learn whatever they needed to know to make their lives right together.

The cut on the back of his hand was almost healed. Gazing at it, she could feel his knuckles against her skin, hear his voice murmuring things in her ear. She smiled, her chest aching at the sight of him perched on a bar stool talking to her fish.

She moved finally, a little unsteadily, toward him, and rested a hand on the bar while she slid onto the stool next to him.

His head shot up. The rest of him stayed completely still, one hand on his untouched beer glass.

"Hi," she said.

He let go of the glass and swerved around to face her, but he, too, kept one hand on the bar, as if for balance. He had on a clean T-shirt, the soft material clinging to every bulge and hollow of his chest, the bright white color a stark contrast to his scuffed and worn leather jacket, but it was perfect Max, she thought. A white knight underneath the streetwise exterior.

"Gracie," he said softly, as if he couldn't fathom why she was there.

She could have shown him. She could have thrown herself at him, heart and soul, and left the rest to chemistry, but he deserved more than that. He deserved words, and explanations, and commitment, and honesty. And she wanted to give all of that to him.

"I saw your car outside," she said finally. It was a

pitiful substitute for what she wanted to say, but even that innocuous sentence was hard to squeeze out through her tight throat.

He studied her solemnly, still barely moving. "Did you come in to get Lucifer?"

She shook her head. "No. I came in to get you, Max."

"You did?"

She nodded. His out-of-the-blue grin brought another rush of illogical tears to her eyes, and the only answer she could make had to be preceded by an audible sniffle. "Yes."

"Ah, Gracie." He jumped off his stool, grasped her by the shoulders, and pulled her a few inches up from her stool. Then he stopped, studying her again, unsure about what she'd meant.

"Max," she said, closing her eyes, making herself say the words aloud. "I want you back. I want us to be together. I don't want a div—"

The words were cut off by his mouth on hers, by his arms pulling her against him, rocking her back and forth and half turning her around until his backside rested on her bar stool and he was kissing her with wild, exuberant abandon.

Restless hearts, the juke box sang, *hold still for love*. But not theirs. Grace's arms circled his shoulders, her hands plunged into his hair, her knee pressed against his leg as he leaned with feet widespread and pulled her closer, closer, kissing her hard, breaking it off only to grin at her again, joyous and wide and a little smug.

She smiled back at him. "You didn't let me finish, Max. I had a whole speech ready to give you."

"Nah," he said. "No speeches. I don't need any speeches. I just need you to not say that word again, okay?"

"What word?"

"The D-I-V word," the bartender said, behind Max's shoulder.

Grace gave him a startled glance. He grinned at her and moved Max's beer glass back on the bar out of harm's way.

Max glanced over his shoulder, but then turned to Grace and gave her a smile as wide as the antlers on the moose above the bar. "Hey, Gracie, guess what?"

"What?"

"We're gonna have a baby."

"Is that so?"

"Yeah. We're gonna be parents. We're gonna drive a minivan, and buy a bunch of tricycles, and start a college fund. And . . . I don't know, take vitamins, see an obstetrician . . ."

She smiled. "We've already done that, Max."

"We have?"

She nodded.

His smile widened again. "Parents," he said. "And we're gonna be good at it. You know that? Especially you, Gracie. Especially you."

"Oh, Max. You're going to be good at it too."

"Yeah?" He grinned again. "I've never been pregnant before," he murmured, moving in closer.

A bubble of mirth and other stray emotions tickled

her in the throat, making her laugh. "I think you're going to have a knack for it, though, Max. You look . . . glowing."

His smile came closer, touched her mouth, then settled, slowly this time, carefully, sensually, into a kiss. Grace's eyes slid closed, and she gave herself up to it, leaning against Max, oblivious to their surroundings or their audience, until a smattering of applause and murmured approvals made her blink, glance around, and give an abashed grin to their neighbors.

"Hey, Grace?" Max whispered in her ear. "Let's go home."

She nodded. "Yes. Let's go home."

"Hey, buddy?" the bartender called as Max circled her waist and started guiding her toward the door. "You want your fish?"

Max took two steps back, gathered up the punch bowl in one arm, and tightened the other one around his wife. "Yeah," he said, speaking to her, "we're keeping the fish. He's family."

THE EDITORS' CORNER

Have no fear, spring is here, bringing with it four April LOVESWEPTs to help ward off the last vestiges of winter. April also brings back four of your favorite authors weaving love stories filled with excitement and danger, honor and trust, romance and passion, just for you. Our courageous heroines and their gorgeous male counterparts must overcome many obstacles to get to that happy ending. Join them on their journeys to happily ever after!

A houseful of kids brings a family together in Marcia Evanick's first installment of her **WHITE LACE & PROMISES** trilogy, **DADDY MATE-RIAL,** LOVESWEPT #830. For weeks Adam Young has been on a desperate mission—to find the woman with whom he'd shared the most passionate night of his life. After watching Emily Pierce frolicking with her children, Adam realizes his most difficult task will be wooing a woman whose heart belongs to her kids. Emily doesn't want to play Cinderella to Adam's Prince Charming, but can she ignore his promises of forever? Marcia brings together a prince of a guy with a pretty young widow in a celebration of delicious fun and touching joy that will renew your faith in happily ever afters.

SILENT WARRIOR John McShane senses the desperation in Cali Ellis's plea for help in LOVE-SWEPT #831, by Donna Kauffman. Now, after he had flown to the Caribbean to rescue her, Cali refuses to leave without answers, and John finds that she still has the power to ignite his desire. John had been Cali's anchor when grief shattered her heart, but could a hero rugged enough to haunt a woman's dreams convince this defiant beauty that he'd fight to keep her forever? In a sexy tale of breathless pursuit and irresistible danger, Donna Kauffman throws this fierce warrior and his ladylove into the fires of restless passion and ultimate possession.

Suzanne Brockmann steams up the pages, as Kayla Grey and Cal Bartlett fight an undeniable attraction that is so right, yet so **FORBIDDEN**, LOVE-SWEPT #832. Sure, Kayla was saved from a drenching storm by a man who'd given her shelter, but did that merit the reckless urge to kiss the handsome cowboy? Cal can't believe he nearly made love with the woman who'd betrayed his brother's memory, but shame wars with desire when Kayla insists that Liam might still be alive. Can a man who's tasted paradise sacrifice the woman he loves? Suzanne answers that question in this sensual tale of honor, trust, and the forbidden fruits of love.

RaeAnne Thayne lets the sparks fly when Andrea

McPhee and Will Tanner fall **IN TOO DEEP**, LOVESWEPT #833. Andrea can't resist teasing Sheriff Tanner about his roadside manner after he stops her for speeding on a Wyoming back road. The sassy rebel gets under Will's skin, seeping through the barriers he's erected to protect his heart from the sorrows of the past. Driven by vengeance and a desire he cannot define, Will softens when Andrea confesses her own demons of grief and loss. Together they each must learn to let go of the past and to seek sanctuary in the love of a lifetime. RaeAnne Thayne writes with wrenching emotion and tender humor in a story of healing hearts and second chances.

Happy reading!

With warmest wishes,

Shauna Summers

Joy Abella

Shauna Summers   Joy Abella

Editor   Administrative Editor

P.S. Look for these Bantam women's fiction titles coming in March. In **A THIN DARK LINE**, the boundaries between the law and justice and love and murder are crossed in the newest hardcover from the *New York Times* bestselling author of GUILTY AS

SIN, Tami Hoag. Hailed by *Rave Reviews* as "a genre superstar," Elizabeth Thornton returns with **THE BRIDE'S BODYGUARD,** a novel about a mysterious stranger and a young woman who believes she's eluded a neglectful guardian's clutches. In **PLACES BY THE SEA,** highly acclaimed author Jean Stone explores the choices that a woman who has everything she could ever ask for must face—until she learns that true love is what she really wants. And immediately following this page, preview the Bantam women's fiction titles on sale *now*!

For current information on Bantam's women's fiction, visit our new web site, *Isn't It Romantic,* at the following address: **http://www.bdd.com/romance**

Don't miss these extraordinary books
by your favorite Bantam authors

On sale in February:

LONG AFTER
MIDNIGHT
by Iris Johansen

THE SCOTSMAN
WORE SPURS
by Patricia Potter

LONG AFTER MIDNIGHT
BY IRIS JOHANSEN

An explosive new hardcover novel of suspense
by bestselling author
Iris Johansen

*Research scientist Kate Denby is on the verge of a major
medical breakthrough that could save countless lives. But
there's someone who doesn't want her to finish her work.
Someone not interested in holding out hope—but in buying
and selling death.*

She didn't look like a warrior, sitting there on the
boy's bed, Ishmaru thought in disappointment. She
looked soft and womanly, without spirit or worth.

He peered through the narrow slit afforded by the
venetian blinds covering the window of the boy's
room.

Look at me. Let me see your spirit.

She didn't look at him. Didn't she know he was
there, or was she scorning his threat to her?

Yes, that must be it. His power was so great tonight, he felt as if the stars themselves must feel it.
Coup always brought added strength and exultation
in its wake. The little girl had felt his power even
before his hands had closed around her throat. The
woman must be taunting him by pretending she was
not aware he was watching her.

His hands tightened on the glass cutter in his
hand. He could cut through the glass and show her he
could not be ignored.

No, that was what she wanted. Even though he was quick, he would be at a disadvantage. She sought to lure him to his destruction as a clever warrior should do.

But he could be clever too. He would wait for the moment and then strike boldly in full view of these sheep with whom she surrounded herself.

And before she died, she would admit how great was his power.

Joshua remained awake for almost an hour, and even after his eyes finally closed, he slept fitfully.

It was just as well they were going away for a while, Kate thought. Joshua wasn't a high-strung child, but what he'd gone through was enough to unsettle anyone.

Phyliss's door was closed, Kate noted when she reached the hall. She should probably get to bed too. Not that she'd be able to sleep. She hadn't lied to Joshua: she was nervous and uneasy . . . and bitterly resentful. This was her home, it was supposed to be a haven. She didn't like to think of it as a fortress.

But, like it or not, it was a fortress at the moment and she'd better make sure the soldiers were on the battlements. She checked the lock on the front door before she moved quickly toward the living room. She would see the black-and-white from the picture window.

Phyliss, as usual, had drawn the drapes over the window before she went to bed. The cave instinct, Kate thought as she reached for the cord. Close out the outside world and make your own. She and Phyliss were in complete agree—

He was standing outside the window, so close they were separated only by a quarter of an inch of glass.

Oh God. High concave cheekbones, long black straight hair drawn back in a queue, beaded necklace. It was him . . . Todd Campbell . . . Ishmaru . . .

And he was smiling at her.

His lips moved and he was so near she could hear the words through the glass. "You weren't supposed to see me before I got in, Kate." He held her gaze as he showed her the glass cutter in his hand. "But it's all right. I'm almost finished and I like it better this way."

She couldn't move. She stared at him, mesmerized.

"You might as well let me in. You can't stop me."

She jerked the drape shut, closing him out.

Barricading herself inside with only a fragment of glass, a scrap of material . . .

She heard the sound of blade on glass.

She backed away from the window, stumbled on the hassock, almost fell, righted herself.

Oh God. Where was that policeman? The porch light was out, but surely he could see Ishmaru.

Maybe the policeman wasn't there.

Didn't Michael tell you about bribery in the ranks.

The drape was moving.

He'd cut the window.

"Phyliss!" She ran down the hall. "Wake up." She threw open Joshua's door, flew across the room, and jerked him out of bed.

"Mom?"

"Shh, be very quiet. Just do what I tell you, okay?"

"What's wrong?" Phyliss was standing in the doorway. "Is Joshua sick?"

"I want you to leave here." She pushed Joshua toward her. "There's someone outside." She hoped he was still outside. Christ, he could be in the living room by now. "I want you to take Joshua out the back door and over to the Brocklemans."

Phyliss instantly took Joshua's hand and moved toward the kitchen door. "What about you?"

She heard a sound in the living room. "*Go*. I'll be right behind you."

Phyliss and Joshua flew out the back door.

"Are you waiting for me, Kate?"

He sounded so close, too close. Phyliss and Joshua could not have reached the fence yet. No time to run. Stop him.

She saw him, a shadow in the doorway leading to the hall.

Where was the gun?

In her handbag on the living room table. She couldn't get past him. She backed toward the stove. Phyliss usually left a frying pan out to cook breakfast in the morning. . . .

"I told you I was coming in. No one can stop me tonight. I had a sign."

She didn't see a weapon but the darkness was lit only by moonlight streaming through the window.

"Give up, Kate."

Her hand closed on the handle of the frying pan. "Leave me *alone*." She leaped forward and struck out at his head with all her strength.

He moved too fast but she connected with a glancing blow.

He was falling. . . .

She streaked past him down the hall. Get to the purse, the gun.

She heard him behind her.

She snatched up the handbag, lunged for the door, and threw the bolt.

Get to the policeman in the black-and-white.

She fumbled with the catch on her purse as she streaked down the driveway toward the black-and-white. Her hand closed on the gun and she threw the purse aside.

"He's not there, Kate," Ishmaru said behind her. "It's just the two of us."

No one was in the driver's seat of the police car.

She whirled and raised the gun.

Too late.

He was on her, knocking the gun from her grip, sending it flying. How had he moved so quickly?

She was on the ground, struggling wildly.

She couldn't breathe. His thumbs were digging into her throat.

"Mom." Joshua's agonized scream pierced the night.

What was Joshua doing here? He was supposed to be— "Go away, Josh—" Ishmaru's hands tightened, cut off speech. She was dying. She had to move. The gun. She had dropped it. On the ground . . .

She reached out blindly. The metal of the gun hilt was cool and wet from the grass.

She wasn't going to make it. Everything was going black.

She tried to knee him in the groin.

"Stop fighting," he whispered. "I've gone to a great deal of trouble to give you a warrior's death."

Crazy bastard. The hell she'd stop fighting.

She raised the gun and pressed the trigger.

*"Charming humor, page-turning intrigue,
and characters so real they step out of the page.
A winner."*
—Iris Johansen, *New York Times* bestselling author
of *THE UGLY DUCKLING*

THE SCOTSMAN
WORE SPURS

BY PATRICIA POTTER

*Andrew Cameron, a penniless Scottish earl, comes to
America seeking a simple life. But he soon finds himself
rescuing a wealthy rancher and hiring on as a cattle
drover. A scrawny, scruffy young boy joins the drive, but
Drew quickly discovers that behind the facade is beautiful
Gabrielle Parker, out to find her father's killer.*

Drew ignored the hooting from the two cowboys riding with him as he gingerly—very gingerly—picked
himself up from the ground.

The fall was ignominious. He couldn't ever remember falling from a horse before. Horsemanship
was one of the few accomplishments he claimed—that
and gaming.

Kirby had warned him that cutting horses were
unlike any other animal, their movements quick and
sometimes unexpected when they saw a cow wandering off. The pinto Drew was riding had done just
that, moving sharply when he'd just relaxed after a
very long day in the saddle.

"Uncle Kirby said you could ride," Damien

Kingsley said nastily. "What other tall tales did you hand him?"

Drew forced a wry smile to his face. He had been the butt of unending razing since he'd first gone on the Kingsley payroll a week earlier. His Scottish accent and unfamiliarity with cattle hadn't helped the image of tenderfoot.

"What do they have for horses in Scotland?" another man scoffed.

Damien, sitting a small roan, snickered. "You ain't going to be any use at all."

Drew tested his limbs. They seemed whole, if sore. He eyed the pinto with more than a little asperity, and the bloody beast bared its teeth as if laughing. Damn, but every bone in his body ached. He had raced horses, had ridden them long distances, but sitting in a saddle eighteen hours a day for a week strained even his experienced muscles. The thought of three months of this shriveled his soul.

Learn cow. That's what Kirby called learning the cattle business. In some strange ungrammatical way, the expression fit. But Drew was beginning to think he'd just as soon jump off the edge of the earth. He'd had no experience with cattle in Scotland, and his enthusiasm for being a cattle baron now had dimmed to the faint flicker of a dying candle.

Yet he'd never been a quitter, and he didn't much like the idea of starting now, nor did he want to see the triumph spreading across Damien's and his brother's faces. Even less did he want to disappoint Kirby.

He started for the pinto.

"Well, lookit that, will ya!" The exclamation came from a drover called Shorty, and all looked out in the direction the man pointed. Drew's own gaze followed the pointing arm.

Drew saw the most moth-eaten, woebegone, and decrepit beast he'd ever had the misfortune to see. Perched precariously on its bony back sat a small figure whose hat was as decrepit as the horse he rode.

"Mebbe Scotty could ride that," one of the men said, laughing uproariously at his own joke and using the name the other drovers had given Drew.

Drew would have loved to cram that laughter down his throat, along with his hat, but that would just make trouble for Kirby. He wondered how long he could curb a temper that had never been known for its temperance.

Then he watched, with the others, the slow approach of the rider.

The boy was enveloped by a coat much too big for him, and only a portion of his face was visible. Under the dirty slouch hat, a pair of dark blue eyes seemed to study him before they lowered and moved on to the other riders before going blank.

"I'm looking for the foreman," he mumbled in a voice that seemed to be changing.

"What for?" one of the men said, using his elbow to nudge a companion. "Want to sell that fine horse of yours? The fellow near the pinto may be interested."

Guffaws broke out again, and the boy's eyes went back to Drew, resting there for a moment. "Lookin' for a job," he said, ignoring the jibe. "Heard they might be hirin' here."

"Pint-size cowboys?" Damien said. "You heard wrong. We're full hired. More than full hired," he added, tossing a disagreeable look at Drew.

"Read about the drive in the newspaper," the boy

said. "It said they be needing help. I want to see the foreman."

Drew admired the boy's persistence, especially in light of the snickers that had just been transferred from himself to the lad. But the drive *was* full hired. A number of much more promising looking cowboys had been turned down. He himself wouldn't have had a chance of hiring on, even at the miserly wage of fifty dollars and keep, had he not been Kirby's friend. It seemed every cowboy in the West wanted to ride with Kirby Kingsley on what was being called a historic drive.

"I'll take you," Drew said. "Follow me."

He took the reins of his horse and limped toward the corral where Kirby was making a final selection of horses to take. There would be ten horses per man, one hundred and eighty mounts in all, not including the sixteen mules designated for the two wagons that would accompany them.

"Mr. Kingsley?" He had stopped calling Kingsley by his first name when he went into his employ, especially around the other men. He had no wish to further aggravate their resentment toward the Scottish tenderfoot.

Kirby turned around, noticed his limp and gave him a grimace that passed for a smile. "Told you about those cutting horses."

"So you did," Drew said wryly. "I won't make the mistake of underestimating them again."

"Good. Nothing broken, I take it."

"Only my pride."

Kirby's lips twitched slightly, then his gaze went over to the boy. "That a horse, boy?"

The boy flushed, and the chin raised defiantly.

"He has heart. Just 'cause no one ever took care of him . . ."

Kirby's smile disappeared. "You have a point. What's your name?"

"Gabe. Gabe Lewis."

"And what's your business?"

"I heard you was hiring."

"Men," Kirby said. "Not boys."

"I'm old enough."

"What? Fourteen? Fifteen?"

"Sixteen," the boy said angrily, "and I've been making my own way these past three years."

"You ever been on a drive?"

The boy hesitated, and Drew could almost see the wheels turning inside his head. He wanted to lie. He would have lied if he hadn't thought he might be caught in it. "No, but I'm a real fast learner."

"We don't need any more hands," Kirby said, turning away. The easy dismissal brought a deeper flush to the boy's face.

"Mr. Kingsley?"

Kingsley swung back around, irritation deepening the lines in his face. He waited for the boy to continue.

The boy's voice became a plea. "I'll do anything, Mr. Kingsley. Maybe I'm not so big, but I'm a real hard worker."

Kirby shook his head.

"I need the job real bad," the boy said in one last desperate plea.

"By the looks of that horse, I'd agree," Drew said helpfully. Strangely enough, he sensed his help wasn't welcome. The boy's gaze cut to his only for a briefest second, but there was no missing the scowl in them.

Kirby looked thoughtful for a moment. "Pepper,

our cook, was complaining yesterday about his rheumatism. Maybe we could use someone to help him out. You up to being a louse, boy?"

"A louse?" The boy's eyes widened, and Drew noticed again how very blue they were.

"A cook's helper," Kirby explained. "A swamper. Clean up dishes, hunt cow chips, grind coffee. You ever done any cooking?"

"Of course," the boy said airily. Drew sensed bravado, and another lie, but Kirby didn't seem to notice. From the moment the boy had mentioned he was desperate, the rancher had softened perceptibly. Drew saw it, noted it. And it surprised him. There was nothing soft about Kirby Kingsley.

He knew, despite the fact he had saved Kirby's life, that if he couldn't pull his own weight he would be gone. His job had been based on the fact that Kirby had seen him shoot—and ride—and believed the rest would come easily enough.

If painfully.

But this slip of a boy sat a horse like a beginner, and he obviously lied about his ability to cook. Those dark blue eyes darted around just enough to say so. And he didn't look strong enough to control a team of four mules. Drew's eyes went to the numerous—but odd—bits and pieces of clothing; it was too hot for so much clothing, which meant he was trying to conceal a thin frame or feared someone would take what little he had if he didn't keep them close to his person.

But if Kirby had noted all these things, and Drew was sure he had because little escaped the man, he made no mention of them.

"My cook has to agree," Kirby was telling the

boy. "If he does, I'll pay you twenty dollars and found."

The boy nodded.

"You can't cut it, you're gone," Kirby added.

The boy nodded again.

"You don't have much to say, do you?" Kirby asked.

"Didn't know that was important." It was an impertinent reply, one Drew might have made himself, and he took another look at the boy's face.

There was no stubble, but the lad's skin was darkened by the sun and none too clean. But then the cook was none too fastidious himself, although Kirby proclaimed his food the best among cattle-drive cooks. That distinction appeared dubious at best—at least to Drew. Texas beef, he'd discovered, was tough and stringy, and the Kirbys' Mexican cook at home spiced it with hot peppers. He wondered if Pepper did the same, and he briefly longed for a piece of fresh salmon or good Scottish lamb.

He quickly discarded the thought. He doubted he would ever return to Scotland, where few of his memories were happy ones. If he had to suffer tough, tasteless beef to banish them, he would consider it more than a good trade.

"Drew?"

Kirby's sharp question broke his rambling throughts and he turned his attention to the man next to him.

"Get the kid some food. I'll talk to Pepper."

"I need to take care of my horse," the boy said. "Give him some oats if you got any."

"I'm Drew Cameron," he said.

The boy looked at him suspiciously and without warmth. "You talk funny."

"I'm from Scotland," Drew explained. "The other hands call me Scotty."

The boy didn't look satisfied, but didn't ask any more questions, either. Instead, still hunched in the coat, he followed Drew into the barn and then into a stall. Drew found some oats and poured them into a feed bucket. The horse looked at him with soft, grateful eyes, and he understood the boy's attachment. Hell, he'd had a horse he'd loved. Too much. Bile filled his throat as he remembered.

"I can take care of him alone," the boy said rudely.

"You got a name for this horse?"

"Billy, if it's any of your business."

"Hell of a name for a horse."

"It ain't your horse."

"No," Drew conceded as he watched the boy take off the bit, then the saddle. He struggled with it, and not just because the saddle was heavy. There was no deftness that comes with practice. His gaze went to the boy's hands. Gloves covered them. New gloves.

And the clothes were fairly new though some effort had been extended to hide that fact. Dirt was too uniform for it to have been accumulated naturally, and the denim trousers were still stiff, not soft and pliant. Something else didn't ring true. The "ain't," perhaps. Drew had an ear for nuances of sounds.

The natural skill had been invaluable in gaming; he could always detect a false note: desperation, bluffing, fear. He thought he detected all three now.

Why? Unless the boy had something to hide other than a need for a job. Could he be a runaway, or something else? Something more ominous?

Drew hadn't forgotten the ambush nor the possibility that someone might try again. And he remembered the ambusher's words. *That little guy.* He very much doubted this slip of a boy could be involved, but he had seen danger and dynamite come in much smaller packages.

He immediately dismissed the idea as quickly as it flitted through his mind. Those last few months in Scotland had raised his caution. A man he'd never suspected—a trainer of horses—had proved to be a murderer and kidnapper. Many things, and people, had not been as they seemed.

"Where are you from?" he asked.

The boy's vivid blue gaze bore into his. "Places."

Drew grinned. It was an answer he'd given frequently. He merely nodded. The boy's business was his own until proved otherwise.

"The bunkhouse is the next building. Take any that doesn't look occupied," Drew said. He'd moved to the bunkhouse himself. There were several empty cots.

"When do we leave?"

Drew heard an anxious note in the boy's voice.

"In two days," Drew said.

"What do you do?" the boy asked unexpectedly, his eyes narrowing.

Drew shrugged. "Just a cowhand," he said, "and if I want to stay that way, I'd better get back to work." He turned, oddly discomfited by the hostility in the boy's vivid blue eyes.

What the bloody hell, anyway. The lad was none of his business.

On sale in March:

A THIN DARK LINE
by *Tami Hoag*

THE BRIDE'S BODYGUARD
by **Elizabeth Thornton**

PLACES BY THE SEA
by *Jean Stone*

DON'T MISS THESE FABULOUS
BANTAM WOMEN'S FICTION TITLES

On Sale in February

LONG AFTER MIDNIGHT

by New York Times *bestselling author* IRIS JOHANSEN

Research scientist and single mother Kate Denby is very close to achieving a major medical breakthrough. But there is someone who will stop at nothing to make sure she never finishes her work. Now Kate must find a way to protect her son and make that breakthrough. Because defeating her enemy could mean saving millions of lives—including the lives of those who mean the most to her.   ____ 09715-6 $22.95/$29.95

THE SCOTSMAN WORE SPURS

by PATRICIA POTTER

"One of the romance genre's finest talents."
—*Romantic Times*

Andrew Cameron, Earl of Kinloch, comes to America to forge a new life and suddenly finds himself employed as a cattle drover. Scrawny, scruffy young Gabe Lewis joins the drive too, sparking Drew's compassion. Then, under the grime and baggy clothes, Drew uncovers beautiful Gabrielle Parker acting the role of her life—to unmask her father's killer.   ____ 57506-6 $5.99/$7.99
